# BILL

# THUNDER

## THE

# BASTARDIZER

Bill Thunder is your average disaffected, world-weary misanthropic PI. He's been there, done that, seen it all and got it remembered in the minutest, most obsessive detail. But this is a case that sees him tested to his limits.

There's nothing unusual about a missing man... but things are a little more complicated when the missing person happens to share a name with the world's most famous recently-deceased celebrity. While on the hunt for Michael Jackson – a wealthy businessman – Thunder risks life and limb as he trawls the violent underworld of shady dealings and Internet pornography.

BILL

# THUNDER

## THE

# BASTARDIZER

2010

Clinicality Press

York, England

First published 2009 by Clinicality Press, York
This edition published 2010
A Clinicality Press Pocket Edition
http://clinicalitypress.co.uk


ISBN 978-0-9556939-5-3

# 1

Sex and money. Ultimately, everything can be boiled down to either one or the other, or a combination of the two in infinitely varying proportions. Love? That's just a variation of the sex aspect of life. When it isn't, it's about money, and that's not exactly love in the strictest sense. Humans: we're simple creatures, although some humans are more simple than others. Me, I'm not so simple, but I like to try to keep things simple. There's no point in complicating matters. Life's complicated enough. The varying blends of sex and money are usually far too complicated, way more complicated than they need to be.

The name's Thunder. Bill Thunder. Some refer to me as The Bastardizer. They can call me what the fuck they like, it doesn't make any difference to me. It's my job to try to simplify things. I get hired by people whose lives are complicated. I get contracted to make things simpler, one way or another. Whatever it takes. They pay me. Money. The sex I can live without, because sex usually complicates things. I don't need complications. My job's complicated enough, so I need to try to keep things simple. Doesn't mean I don't necessarily ever get any sex along the way, though.

Other details about me aren't important. Only the barest, most essential facts are needed here. I'm The Bastardizer, and I do my job for money. Sometimes I get sex. But I keep business and pleasure separate. It's the only way. What more do you need? My age, my physical appearance, you don't need them. In fact, I need them to be kept only for me. It's easier for me to do my job if I can remain anonymous.

I don't care how that makes you feel. Feelings only complicate matters. Let's stick with the facts. The facts are the only things that matter. This is my story.

Tuesday August 12th, 11:02.53: an ordinary day at the office. What constitutes an ordinary day is classified information. But who cares about classified? Let's stick to the facts. The fact is that it doesn't matter, you don't need to know. I'm sitting in my chair, reading through some files. Cases ready to be closed. The phone rings. Twice. I pick up.

'W. T. P. D. A.' That's the William Thunder Private Detective Agency.

'Hello…' a female voice. Mid to late thirties, at a guess. 'Is that the detective's agency?'

'Yes.'

'Thunder's?'

'Yes.'

'I… I'm wanting to speak to Mr. Thunder.' She speaks hesitantly. Nervous, by the sound of it.

'Who's calling?'

'Erm, my name's Mrs. Johnson.'

'Who gave you this number?' It's on-line, but it's only in certain selected directories. You won't find me in the Yellow Pages, that's for sure. Not least of all because it costs to list in there and on Yell.com. But it's not all about the money. You can never be too careful in this business. Some people would call it paranoia. But in this line of business, it's just self-preservation. Gotta watch your back. You never know who's watching or who's behind you.

She hesitates. 'A… a friend gave me your card. I'd really rather not say who…'

'Okay, fair enough.'

'So can I speak to Mr. Thunder? It's just… I need to speak to him. *It's important.*'

She sounded desperate. She could be a phoney, but at this juncture she'd be the only one disclosing sensitive information, so I figured I should give her the green light.

'You're speaking to him now. Go ahead, Mrs. Johnson.'

'You do detective work, yes?'

'It's certainly within my remit, yes.'

'I think I may have a job for you,' she says.

I prick up my ears. 'Go on.'

She hesitates. 'I can't discuss it here. I may be under surveillance.' That makes two of us. Sure, you can call me paranoid. Maybe I am. Doesn't mean I've not got reason to be.

'Ah. Okay. Where are you?'

'I'm at home. But I'm heading out shortly. I have an appointment.'

'Okay.' She's not giving me much. 'So how can I help?' I ask.

'Could we meet up?'

'Sure.'

'Where's good?' she asks

'You choose. I'm mobile,' I tell her.

She made her suggestion. It sounded safe. Public enough for her in case I wasn't kosher, secluded enough for her to give the slip to anyone trailing her, or at least so she hoped. Me, I wasn't too bothered. I can disappear into the background or fade into any crown in the blink of an eye. I scribbled down the details of my assignation. She wanted to meet the same day at 15:00 hours. She must have been desperate. Or very impatient. Either way, I wouldn't have long to find out.

'See you then.'

'You will,' I say.

'You will be there, won't you?' she sounds panicked.

'Absolutely,' I assure her. 'Reliability and discretion are what I stake my reputation on. And being a damn good detective,' I add. 'No stone unturned.'

'Thank you.'

She hangs up.

Her vagueness and the tone of panic, of confusion in her voice don't surprise me one bit. The majority of women who call me do so in a state of desperation. And most of my clients are women. For some reason, guys seem more reluctant to hire private investigators. Maybe they prefer to do the digging themselves. Maybe they think they can do a better job, and that to hire someone undermines their masculinity. Fine, whatever. In my experience, most men are pricks. All ego and machismo and no balls. Me, I got balls of steel, the size of watermelons.

I left the office at 14:12. I had to allow plenty of time for my journey. Rule number 3: when travelling, never go by a direct route. This rule only applies to this line of work, you understand. What are rules 1 and 2? Later: information should only ever be disclosed on a need-to-know basis. Travelling by any route usually takes me longer than most, because I'm at the mercy of public transport and my own steam. You might think that odd, given that I try to leave nothing to chance, but it isn't. While public transport timing may be a little less than perfect on many occasions, it's far safer for a guy like me to travel that way. If I owned a car, there would be a chance, a very good one at that, that someone would identify me by my vehicle type, colour, plates. There are people who would want to wipe me out. It's far easier to be anonymous on a bus or a train and taking a different route each time than it is driving around in the same car all the time. You know it makes sense.

2

14:57, I stroll into The Grapes on Beaumont Street, extinguishing my cigarette as I reach the door. Today's the day I quit. An average modern pub in every way. Late twentieth century construction, wooden door propped open, cavernous open-plan interior, polished wooden floor, carpeted seated areas around the edges, long bar of polished mahogany bristling the best part of a dozen electric pumps and not a single hand-pump. Mainline spirits on optics at the back of the bar which is lined with mirrors and a huge fridge full of white wine, mostly Chardonnay and Pinot Grigiot. A guy and a chick behind the bar in black and white uniforms. He has dark wavy hair and stubble, she's bleached blonde, slightly chubby. Looks a little slutty.

I take a glance round, not in search of my potential client, but in case I see anyone who might be out for me. It could be a set-up, after all. I've been set up a few times in the past and only just lived to tell the tale. Of course, this means that I've learned the hard way to tell the likelihood of a set-up, and this didn't have any of the common signs. Even so, you can't be too careful. So I glance round, but subtly. Looking furtive or anxious can arouse suspicion and almost certainly draws attention. In this line of work there's no such thing as 'the wrong kind' of attention, either. Any attention is bad. Invisibility is the desired state. I've got pretty good at doing invisible, or at least as near as dammit. The trick is always to see them before they see you.

I make straight for the bar. Looking like you're uncertain – about anything – can be dangerous, a real giveaway.

'Good afternoon, sir,' says the barboy. He's not a man: he can't be a day over twenty-one. At least he's attentive, even if he isn't all that smartly presented.

'Afternoon,' I reply.

'What'll it be, sir?' he asks.

I'm tempted to say that it'd be a good start if he dropped the 'sir' shit. I've not been knighted, and don't expect to be anytime soon, or ever. Still, better he's polite than telling me to fuck off out of the establishment or otherwise calling security. Wouldn't be the first time that's happened to me.

I don't hesitate. No change of a beer so it's straight to the hard stuff. 'Jack Daniel's,' I tell him. 'Straight.'

Cliché I know, but there you have it. I'm a cliché.

The bargirl looks over. I can't tell if she's being surprised so be selling neat spirits at three in the afternoon, if she's impressed by my hardness or just curious because she's bored out of her tiny bottle-blonde mind.

Deciding whether to remain at the bar or to find a table at the farthest corner while still being able to watch both the bar and the door simultaneously is often an important one. I figured that remaining at the bar was the best strategy for this one. She sounded nervous, and might not show, but assuming she would, she'd probably not want to peer around looking for me, and I obviously have no clue as to what she looks like.

Still, this was her chosen venue and it was pretty quiet, so however invisible I made myself she'd still have little difficulty finding me at the bar. If she was a regular, she'd know me by virtue of the fact she didn't recognise me.

I was feeling a little tense, and although I've had a lot of practice with countless steak-outs over the years, I'm lousy when it comes to killing time. 15:13:52 and no-one else has come into the place and so my glass is dry. Sitting with my back to the room, I can see the rest of the patrons in the mirror behind the bar. There are only half a dozen people in: a couple of executive type men in their mid-forties dressed in pinstripe suits with brown brogues and silk ties, and a cluster of four – three guys and a girl, who look and sound like Spanish tourists. No Mrs. Johnsons here.

I look up and glance over to the bar staff. They're chatting away about mobile phones and games consoles and don't notice me at first. I know better than to wave or click my fingers. I've come to learn that if you look at someone long enough, they'll somehow become aware of the fact. Like some sixth sense. They stop their chatter and look at me. The girl steps forward this time.

'Same again, sir?' she asks cheerfully.
'Please,' I nod.
'What was it?' she queries. Bint.
'J.D.,' I say.
'Coke?'
'No, straight,' I tell her.
'Ice?'

'No, straight,' I tell her.

I couldn't help clocking her arse when she turned to get the drink. Not bad. She clicked the shot from the optic and placed the drink in front of me. I handed her a £5 note and received less change than I would have hoped.

I took a hit of the liquor and sat, pondering, staring into the mirrors. Would Mrs. Johnson show? I'd give her till half past then cut my losses and either return to the office or find a decent pub where I could get a proper pint.

Just then, a woman walked into the bar. She was quite smartly dressed, in a pencil skirt that came just below the knee. Her calves were slim, their shape defined by her wearing 3" heels. Shoulder-length brunette hair with what appeared to be a slight natural wave. Not too much makeup, and applied in a way that complimented her natural skin tones. She approached the bar slightly hesitantly, but carried herself with what looked to me like a forced air of confidence. She orders a glass of medium white wine and looks around rather anxiously.

She clocks me as she's being handed her change. Trying to look discreet and failing miserably, she sidles over, fumbling to return her change to her brown snakeskin-effect purse.

'Mr. Ch, Thunder?' she stammers, looking more at the bar than me. 15:23. She's almost half an hour late but I'm not about to raise the issue and she's not about to explain or apologise.

'Guilty as charged,' I nod nonchalantly.

'I wasn't sure if...' she begins uncertainly.

'No worries,' I tell her, emollient,

placatory. 'Shall we go and sit somewhere a little more, uh, secluded?'

She nods and picks up her glass, on which condensation is forming and beginning to run to the stem. She's perhaps a little younger than I'd envisaged from her voice on the phone, likely early to mid thirties. We head to the farthest recess of this designer airport lounge and take a table. I sink into a leatherette armchair, and she does the same in the seat opposite me. she puts her handbag down beside her and crosses her legs.

'I don't know if you can help me,' she begins, glancing around as though someone may be listening in.'

'I'll see what I can do,' I tell her. It's not that I'm a sucker for a damsel in distress. I'm not flirting here. But I want the job and want the money, so a little courtesy goes a long way in the game of convincing a potential client. Besides, this damsel seems genuinely distressed. 'What's the nature of your problem – what is it you'd like me to help with, precisely?' no point waggledancing round the situation. This is business and I like to conduct it in a businesslike fashion. Quick, clean, efficient.

'It's my husband,' she says, biting her lip. I know it's nerves, but she looks sexy as hell as she does it.

'It usually is,' I reply dryly.

'He's *missing*,' she says, genuine concern on her face and in her voice.

'Uh-huh.' I hear it all the time. Guys fuck off and leave their wives without a word all the time. They usually resurface sooner or later.

'I'm worried,' she persists.

'Not without good reason,' I assure her. 'When did he disappear?'

'A week or so ago,' she replies awkwardly.

'Or so?' I query. Such vagueness really isn't helpful, although it is extremely common. How can someone not know when someone goes missing?

'I'm not exactly sure,' she says, looking somewhat lost.

'Ok,' I say and try a different tack in the hope that I can get something a little more useful from her. 'When did you see him last?'

'Ten days ago' she replies, more confidently. Now we were getting somewhere.

'Not so long,' I muse. I indicate she should continue.

'He went away on business for a few days. I spoke to him on the first night he was away, and got texts from him the next day, then nothing. I wasn't that bothered at first, I know how he gets wrapped up in his busy schedule so I don't always hear from him every day or night while he's away, but after a couple of days when he wasn't picking up or returning my calls or texts I started to worry. I hate snooping but I went through his drawers but couldn't find any reservations so got the details of the hotel he was staying at from his secretary and rang that and they said they'd never heard of him or and hadn't had any rooms booked for the company he works for.'

'And which company is that?' I cut in.

'Well he's currently operating two,' she

says, 'MJ Inc., and 2000 Watts. But he recently started up Tabloid Junkies, a PR company.'

'Great name' I say, half sarcastic, half serious.

'I suggested it,' she says, a smile flickering across her mouth. Her eyes light up momentarily, too. I can't help noticing how pretty they are.

'So it's true what they say?' I spin.

'What that?'

'That behind every great man is a great woman?'

'Oh, well...' she flushes slightly and glances away.

'Anyway, so what happened then?' I say returning to topic.

'Well, I tried with the name of his secretary and manager and his PA and anyone I could think of at the office, but nothing. And yes, I did try with the other company names, even though they're now managed by independent third parties who are contracted to run them on his behalf since he started Tabloid Junkies. I still got nothing.'

She sure could talk, but this was good background, and so I just nodded and grunted occasionally while scribbling notes as fast as I could. I needed all of this info. It might not all be relevant, but you never know what you're going to need to know or when. I might have a good memory, but I'm not a Dictaphone. Notes are essential. Good note-taking skills are essential. I've had years of practice and am a good note-taker. 'What then?' I quiz.

'I started to panic, I thought *Oh my god, what the hell's going on? This is fucking ridiculous!* So I started to get a bit hysterical. The hotel receptionist guy wasn't very helpful, he started getting all snotty and was like *I'm sorry madam, I really can't help you, are you sure you've got the right hotel?* And I was going *yes I'm sure* but I was starting to have doubts, you know? Anyway, I was almost screaming at this point and tried describing him to the guy and he said *I think he's been here, yes, but I think he checked out this morning* and I went a bit nuts then hung up.' She pauses for breath and throws back a long draught of her wine.

Seeing her glass is almost empty, I offer her a refill. Although she was talking, and at nineteen to the dozen, I really needed her to talk a lot more to get a handle on the situation. Why me and not the police? What was the background to her husband's disappearance? A drink generally works as a loosener. Besides, I was ready for another one myself. She accepted. I could write it off against tax as hospitality, and probably tack it onto her bill if I got the business, and it was looking likely. I returned with more drinks and she filled me in with details of the hotel her missing husband was supposed to be staying at, his job, the company he worked for and all that cal before she suddenly clocked her watch.

'I have to go!' she exclaims. 'I have an appointment I can't be late for!'

'Ah...'

'Will you take the case? Please? Help me?' she implores, fixing me with her big brown eyes, the pupils dilated after two large glasses of wine in quick succession.

'You've got me,' I tell her. 'I will need a few more details, and a retainer, though,' I add.

'Oh, oh, yes, of course. How much?'

I hit her with the figure. 'Strictly cash only,' I caution.

'No problem', she replies. She didn't bletch and if the sum surprised her she didn't let on. So she was smartly presented. That didn't mean she was loaded. But she clearly wasn't broke, because I don't come cheap. 'When can I get it to you?'

'Drop it by my office tomorrow' I suggested. I scribbled the address on a piece of paper and handed it to her, along with my card.

'I'm not sure when I'll be free,' she said, casting her eyes down to her black patent leather shoes.

'Call me to arrange a time.'

'Ok, I'll to that,' she confirmed, stuffing the folded sheet and the card into her purse. 'Thank you. Bye.' And then she was gone.

I necked the last of my J.D. 16:11. I couldn't be arsed to go back to the office now. Business was slow and I wanted a beer. I couldn't do anything about this missing bloke until Mrs. Johnson had done furnishing me with the essential details anyway so I knocked off there and then and headed to The Crown down Salinger Lane for some sweet, sweet ale.

## 3

The alarm woke me with a start. 6:15am. Sharp. Same as every other day. It pays to get up and get going. Life's too short for lie-ins. Lie-ins are for pussies and wasters. I'm no pussy and I'm no waster.

I felt like death. I hauled my sorry ass out from under the duvet where it's warm and cozy. I can hear the patter of large drops of water pelting against the bedroom window. Scratching my aching head, I staggered over and part the curtains. I peered out through the space between the heavy lined fabric. The morning is cold – 12°C, with a steady 15mph north-northwesterly, gusting up to 27mph – and wet. The sky's dull, dark. At least the pollen count's low. The rain has been pouring down for hours now. It's August, but to look at it you'd think it was the middle of November. The road outside is sitting under two inches of flood, the pavement glistens and the surfaces of the puddles are covered in ringlets as the heavy raindrops batter down hard.

My churning guts dictate a move into the bathroom. I expel a greasy turd, high in ale-content, into the bowl. Flush, wash hands. That's she shit over. Time to shower and shave. A slice of toast and I'm out in 45 minutes.

I smoke a cigarette and call in at the coffee house a few doors down from the office on my way in. I always head to work on foot, even when it's raining. It's not far, and parking's a pain in the arse.

Besides, as I said, I don't own a car. Not since my last one got bombed. I was supposed to have been in it, but I got wise just in time and the bomber ended up detonating the thing with one of his co-conspirators inside. Result. The fuckers left me alone after that. Most of them are doing time now anyway, no doubt getting anally raped every night. Child killers are never popular in prison, for some reason.

The bus takes forever, taking the most circuitous route imaginable and is full of grannies and council estaters. I swear this city's going downhill fast, and the signs of the country's ageing population are abundant here in Fieldham. So it's quicker to walk, 25 to 30 minutes at my usual pace. Quicker if I jog, although I prefer not to. Plus I can smoke on the way. I'm not in bad shape, considering my age and lifestyle. Yes, I'm wearing pretty well and have grown into my features by all accounts. Not so young, but still ruggedly handsome. I do ok with the ladies. When I get the time. Not that I've had much time recently.

'Tall Americano,' I say to girl behind the counter who looked depressingly chipper in comparison to me.

'Black?'

'Please.'

'Sugar?' I like this place. They not only make decent coffee but save you the grief of having to tear open those annoying little sachets, spilling sugar all over the side and slopping your coffee while some ignorant corporate tosser's jostling you to take a napkin, like you get in so many other places. Some of the female baristas are pretty tasty, too.

'Please. Five,' I say.

She struggles to stifle her surprise.

'Five?' she echoes to check she's heard right. She's clearly new in here. Explains why I don't recognise her. Being as regular a customer as I am, I recognise most of the staff, even though the turnover's pretty high.

'Yep,' I confirm. I can't help but smirk a little bit.

She makes busy preparing my drink and places it on the counter in front of me. I hand her a £5 note and receive less change than I would have liked. Still, she has a nice rack so I drop a couple of coins from the shrapnel she gives me into the tips jar.

'Thank you. Have a good day,' she beams.

'See ya later,' I smile, picking up my coffee and coasting to the door. Back out onto the street. It's still dull. It's still raining. I get the feeling it's going to be one of those days where the coffee's the only good thing about it.

I arrive at the office. It's 7:36. I unlock the door, put my coffee down on the desk and hang my dripping coat on the stand behind the door. Yes, I wear a Gabardine Mac. But only when it's raining. Cliché I know, but there you have it. I'm a cliché.

I fire up the PC. I don't have a lot to do this morning. Just a couple of invoices to send for works completed, but I'm currently caseless. I put this down in part to the recession, and in part to the Internet.

It's so much easier to snoop nowadays. You can do your own detective work, and comparatively cheaply. Spycams and covert surveillance equipment can be obtained quite easily on-line, and it's not hard to get software that tracks people's Internet use, their whereabouts, even their emails and things either. You can even hire hackers now. I don't exactly approve of such methods myself. It's a stalker's paradise. Privacy is pretty much a thing of the past. Hell, you can't even blog anonymously anymore, and they can trace your IP and see where you're logging on. And that's before you even start on the state's legalised spying programme with phone monitoring and email monitoring and CCTV and a DNA database and... It's endless. It's not good for the individual. You'd think I'd be pleased that information's so freely available now, but I'm not. I value my privacy. And besides, having everything out there's bad for business.

I checked my email and then started scanning the news pages once I'd filed the invoices ready to mail out. The coffee was still too hot to drink, somewhere in the region of 190°F.

The phone rang. It was Mrs. Johnson. She'd be over in 15.

15 is actually 25 and I'm learning fast that punctuality isn't her forte. She's elegantly dressed again, looking every bit the businesswoman. She hangs her cashmere coat on the stand and I motion her to one of the spare seats in he Spartan place I call my office. She sits down, crossing her shapely

legs. Her skirt, just above the knee again, is black with a slit that goes halfway up her thigh.

*Stockings or tights?* I wonder for a moment as she delves into her double handle French design Tote bag and draws out a Filofax and executive folder both in expensive-looking matching black leather. From the folder she takes a white self-sealing C5 envelope which she passes to me. it's good quality stationery, heavy paper, 100gsm, watermarked. I notice her breasts – not large but perky, I'm guessing a 34B or C – thrusting against the crisp white fabric of her silk blouse as she leans forward, her hand extended toward me. I take the envelope. So far she's hardy said a word.

'Your retainer, Mr. Thunder,' she says. 'Cash, as requested. It's all there.'

'Thank you,' I reply. It's bad form to count it, so I fight the urge, having been done over more than once.

In return I hand her two copies of my standard contract. She skims through the first and then signs and dates them both.

'I'm really not too bothered about cost,' she says.

Glad to hear it. Not that I'm in the habit of fleecing people and I always record my hours honestly. I abhor hypocrisy and I expect others to be accountable and so by the same rule I ensure I'm accountable. 'I'll let you know if there are likely to be any particularly out of the ordinary expenses incurred,' I assure her. 'It's in the contract anyway.'

'Good, that's fine,' she says in a businesslike but pleasant tone.

'Have you got time for a few more questions?'

'Of course. I'm sorry I had to leave so hastily yesterday,' she apologises.

'Not at all. You're clearly a very busy lady. Goes with the territory of being a professional,' I acknowledge. What sort of professional she is, I haven't a clue, and I'm not about to ask. Not yet. 'First things first. Your husband's name?'

'Mark.'

'Mark Johnson?'

'Yes.' She hesitates. 'No. It's Jackson. His name's Jackson.'

'Right.' Sometimes trying to guard one's privacy is misguided. 'Glad you told me. It helps to know the real name of the person I'm looking for. Are you Jackson too?'

'Yes. He does sometimes use the name Johnson though. It might be useful to know.'

'Highly probable,' I concur, jotting these details in a spiral bound notepad. 'And what does he do?'

Turns out he's a high-flying exec. It makes disappearing harder, but also all the more suspicious. She gives me a brief outline of his business activities and interests, and I take it all down. At least I have a starting point now. She hands me a sheaf of papers in a brown A4 envelope from the folder with the explanation that 'some of these papers might help.' One never knows. Finally she hands me her business card. I frown at the small font bearing the name Jacinta Jackson in a copperplate typeface. The name rings a bell. I don't let on.

'Call me as soon as you have anything, won't you? Day or night. And if you need anything else...'

'I'll be in touch,' I confirm.

She rises and takes her coat. She's at the door, her hand on the handle when she pauses and turns her head.

'Mike,' she says.

'Huh?'

'His name's not Mark. He sometimes calls himself Mark, but his name's actually Mike.'

Am I hearing right? 'As in Michael?'

She flushes slightly, looking vaguely embarrassed. 'Yes.'

'That's what's on his birth certificate?'

'Yes.'

'Right.'

'Please don't laugh,' she pipes, colouring at the cheeks.

'I'm not laughing,' I deadpan.

'Thank you.'

'Think nothing of it.'

'You're a gentleman,' she tells me.

'I like to think so,' I say, exhaling. I could really use a cigarette. 'You do realise how difficult it could prove to hunt down a Michael Jackson?'

'Believe me, I've tried. I didn't run straight to you,' she retorted.

'There aren't many who do,' I carped, a little put out.

'But you'll do it?' she thrusts. 'You'll find my husband?'

'I'll try,' I say. She gives me a look. It's not quite as blatant as a flutter of the eyelashes, but it has the same effect. 'I'll do my best,' I append.

'I can't ask for more, really,' she says, a weary note to her tone. She checks her watch. 'I've really got to go. Good luck. Call me.' And she is gone.

Fuck. So I'm looking for Michael Jackson. John Smith or Joe Bloggs would have been bad, but this is taking the piss. Have I been had?

The moment she's gone, I get myself online and start searching. After I've opened the envelope, counted the cash and shoved it into my wallet, that is. Yes, it's all there. Ok, so I don't expect to find her missing husband on the Internet, sitting around waiting for an IM on Facebook or in some dodgy chat-room used by paedophiles to groom kids, but I can at least do a bit of research and see if Mrs. Johnson's – sorry, Jackson's – story checks out.

It's fucking hard work. Depending on whether or not you frame the search terms in speech marks or not, Googling Michael Jackson used to yield anywhere between (approximately) 32,000,000 and 49,600,000 hits. That all changed when he croaked, of course. Leaped to 35,000,000 to 63,000,000 dependent on whether or not you put the search terms in quotation marks within a couple of hours of the news breaking. By 7am on the 26th June 2009, it was at 37,200,000 or 65,500,000, and three days later it was 49,000,000 or 84,000,000 depending. Within a week, it had hit 50,300,000 / 98,300,000. A month, 200,000,000 / 226,000,000.

Insanity. Nothing like the premature death of a global celebrity to get the media buzzing. So while the Internet makes snooping easier, it can have its downsides.

It takes a lot of narrowing, a lot of experimental permutations of various key words and even more patience to find anything about any Michael Jackson who isn't *the* Michael Jackson, and who also uses various permutations of Mark, Mike and Johnson by way of a name. I quickly calculated six different possible permutations. And that was just based on the three forenames and two surnames I knew of. These pseudonymous types were prone to using far more names than they ever let on as a rule. And my early impression was that Jackson / Johnson had all the traits of a classic confidence trickster. Or a man with something to hide.

I did manage to verify that Jackson had two businesses, and that one – Jackson and Co. – was run by his eldest son, Joe. Who'd have believed it? I called them up and managed to secure an appointment with Jackson Jr.

After lunch, which consisted of a bagel and a large black coffee from the shop along the street from the office, plus three high-tar cigarettes – Marlboro red-top 100s, with 1.0mg nicotine and a lung-busting, alveoli-suffocating 13mg tar, none of this pussy-ass lights shit for me – I made a call to an old friend. As another PI, he should have been competition, and in many ways he was, but we got on well and went way back. We helped one another out from time to time. Other times, we'd just get together, chew the fat and get pissed. And why not?

I dialled and the phone rang out for what felt like an eternity, but was in fact only 11 rings.

'Gash,' the familiar voice snapped brusquely.

'Gash,' I affirmed, then announced myself: 'Thunder.'

'Bill!' Roger exclaimed.

'The very same,' I replied.

I simply wanted a second opinion. He was remarkably well connected in business circles considering he was such a maladjusted, misanthropic, borderline sociopath, and a complete cunt to boot. I quizzed him briefly about Jackson and Co., during which time he confirmed what Mrs. J. had told me and what I'd found on-line, before arranging to meet up for a drink. Or ten. He agreed, and that was that. I rifled through the notes I'd taken while talking to Roger then got back to work researching my case. The Internet certainly takes a lot of the legwork out of this job, and research really is well worth investing time in at the start. It can save a lot of time and energy later. Besides, there wasn't much I could do until I'd spoken to Jackson Jr.

4

The following day is Thursday – 14th August. Just another day, another date, I attach no importance to it. It's 10:15 and I'm just a couple of doors away from Jackson and Co., who reside at 312 Magnolia Street West. I'm early for my appointment with Jackson Jr., who currently co-owns the venture, allegedly. Precisely what he, or the company, do is unclear and unimportant, it's all corporate bullshit. Finance and equity, their business listing says. Swindling in other words. I was unable to ascertain much more from their website or any of my contacts in the city. I'll concede there aren't many. I've gone armed with nothing but a pen, a notepad and my wits, augmented by what information I had gleaned from Roger and from my hours of research the previous day.

There was evidence – mostly anecdotal, from Roger, based on conversations he'd had – that Jackson & Co. had connections to a character by the name of Al Reynolds. I was aware of him, had been in the same room a couple of times, but I had no direct experience of the man. He was a former partner of Jackson & Co, back when it had been a father / son plus supporting cast operation. Reynolds was renowned as an unsavoury individual with his fingers in many pies. Mostly dodgy, of course, but he somehow managed to stay squeaky clean when the pigs had come sniffing round. He was fucking Teflon, that one. Reynolds had supposedly gone it alone – variously reported as an amicable, mutual decision with the Jacksons and as having been a question of did he jump or was he pushed in what was an acrimonious battle of wills. There were indications that it might all have been staged and a smokescreen for something – what was unclear. Guess that means the smokescreen was a success. So my sources said that the Jacksons had kept their connections with Reynolds, who, according to Roger, had also disappeared off the face of the planet in the past couple of weeks, but was, officially 'away on business.'

My priority wasn't Reynolds' shady dealings. I was here to see if there was anything young Jackson could tell me about his father's disappearance and possible whereabouts. I wasn't here to give him a hard time. But if Jackson was bankrolling Reynolds' operation, it's imperative I give him the interrogation he deserves.

I announce my arrival to the bozo on the front desk at 10:18:36 and am advised to take a seat. Jackson keeps me waiting till past due – 10:36:41 to be specific.

I enter the office, decorated a sickly eggshell blue with expensive-looking silver detail that screams 'executive.' I smell Jackson's cologne before I actually catch sight of him. The man is reclining in the immense leather chair behind a bespoke Ercol desk in finest rosewood with walnut inlay. The places reeks of excessive and tasteless opulence. It's needlessly extravagant. And I still haven't a clue what the company does. He rises and gestures me to sit in the seat opposite. He wears a wide pinstripe suit in charcoal grey and a look of disdain, and has a foppish demeanour.

'Welcome,' he oozes, and it's perhaps as well I'm no blennophobe because he's one slimy fuckbucket.

I don't have time for this crapulous coxcombe's smooth bavardage. As I suspected, it's all a façade. No wonder he's known as the 2D Kid in certain circles. The trouble is, he's fucking Teflon, which is why he's still here, and I'm talking to him over his plush desk rather than through bars. He's a smooth criminal, that's for sure. But he's weak, and the moment I begin to squeeze him with some direct questions, he starts to squirm.

'I expect you know why I'm here,' I say.

'My father, I assume,' he slicks, teeth clenched.

'Yes and no.'

'Do indulge me,' he tonks. He speaks with an affected nasal whine. It makes me want to punch him. I suspect he takes it up the arse.

'I was hoping you could indulge me. Your father signed this concern over to you three years ago, yes?'

'That's correct.'

'Why?'

'He gifted it as a means of diffusing his assets and thus reducing the potential Inheritance Tax I would be liable for in the event of his death. He's worth a lot of money. He wanted to pursue a new venture and expected it would do well, but by keeping the two companies separate – and that means separate ownership, the successes or failures of one would not impact on the other. If his new venture was a success, his existing assets – this company – would not be subject to still higher taxation because it's in my hands and therefore technically not his asset. If it was not a success, it would not drag the balance sheet of this company down. It's sound business sense, and all completely above board.'

'Glad to hear it. So he has no interest in this company since signing it over?'

'That's correct.'

'No involvement in this company in any capacity?'

'Right. I mean, I'll ask him for advice, but it's nothing more than that.' He doesn't look at me, and instead picks some imaginary dirt from under his well-manicured index finger.

'So you've never used him in a consultant's capacity? And paid him for this advice and put him on the books as a third party consultant?'

He shifted uncomfortably in his chair. 'No.'

He's lying through his teeth and we both know it. I can't blame him for wanting to remain tight-lipped though. Anything he discloses might prove incriminating, one way or another. His nostrils flare as he twitches his Dilator Naris Anterior and Dilator Naris Posterior. There's a visible pulse in his temple as the blood pumps through his superficial temporal veins. He's clearly adrenalized.

'Ok. And when did you last speak to your father?'

'Late last week, I think.'

'You think? You can do better than that,' I cajole. 'You don't seem particularly interested for a man whose father's just gone missing.'

'He's an adult,' he sneers dismissively, lifting his nose to the air.

'Has he done this sort of thing before?' I press.

'Not that I can recall.'

'So why is it that you don't seem all that concerned? Does he have any enemies you can think of? Anyone who might want him out of the picture? Any affairs?'

The prick prickles at this. 'I don't like what you're insinuating,' he coughs.

'I'm insinuating nothing. I'm simply asking,' I level.

'But you hear it all the time. Men disappear, leave their wives for their secretary, that sort of thing.'

Jackson coughs. There's a sweat breaking on his botoxed brow. He can't be a day over thirty-six. 'Look...' he begins, but I'm warming up here. Time to hit him with a proper barrage.

'Or with their trainers. Y'know, can't come clean about their sexuality so disappear to start a new life in the sun with their gay lover... So, I'll ask you again. what do you know about your father's last known movements, where he was? What can you tell me about the will? And when did you last speak to him?'

'Why can't you just leave me alone?' he whines faggishly.

'And why can't you give a straight answer?'

I shoot back.

He runs his hand down his forehead and over his eyes in a slow anguished move. 'Last Wednesday.'

'Wasn't so hard, was it? So, a week yesterday?'

'Yes.'

'What time?'

'Around 3pm.'

'What did you discuss?'

'Nothing much. He was away on business, trying to get sponsors and the like for his new venture. It wasn't that he lacked the funds to fund it himself, you understand, but any smart businessman knows it's wise to split the costs. Yes, you have to share the profits, but it reduces risk, too.'

'Of course, there are ways to avoid sharing the profits,' I intimate.

'I'm sure I don't know what you mean.' He looks put out.

'I'm sure you do.'

'Well, yes, but not in relation to my father. He was straight up.'

'I'm sure he was.' The double entendre was entirely intentional. The rumours had been rife for years regarding Jackson's less mainstream predilections.

Jackson Jr's eyes narrow. 'Look, if you're just going to come in here and make unfounded insinuations...'

'Don't worry, I'm not,' I assure him.

'Thank you,' he slimes.

'I'm not only here to ask about your father,' I say, making a change of tack.

'Ah.' He turns a shade paler.

'I think you know who, and why,' I press.

'In essence, yes.' His well-oiled hair shimmers in the light. 'More missing persons, I understand... I'm not sure I can tell you anything you don't already know, or anything that I've not already told he police.'

That piqued my interest. As far as I knew, the police hadn't been notified. I'd have to check that out to see if he was telling the truth on that one.

'Which was what?'

'That I knew nothing,' he greased.

'We both know that's not true,' I shot back. 'Unless you know nothing about your own business and finances, too, which I can't believe for a second. You have a reputation for keeping a close eye on your affairs... if you see what I mean.' He'd take the hint.

'Hmm. I see my reputation precedes me.' Smug fuck.

'Yes, you're well known for being hands-on and involved with the day-to-day running of your operations.'

'Ah.'

He's broken into a sweat. His pulse – visible in his temple – has rocketed to 165 BPM, and counting.

'So the transactions into the account of Reynolds won't have escaped your attention,' I press.

He squirms, eyes bugging, almost exophthalmic. Roger's quip that this bozo is 'probably aproctus' springs to mind, and he's probably right.

'Look...' he's wheezing now, a horrible rasping, gurgling sound like a blocked drain. I wonder if his trachea is inflamed or simply contracting spontaneously. I can't help but wonder if he's putting it on.

'I'm looking. And listening.' The little weasel's trying my patience here. I'm tempted to put a hand round that skinny little throat and squeeze the information out of his gasping larynx. I'm tempted to take him apart, but he's of less use to me in pieces so I exercise restraint.

He recovers his breath momentarily, but perspiration is running down his forehead in rivulets. He was flushed. I was clearly rattling the guy. That was proving far easier than I'd expected – just a pity extracting details from him wasn't. But before I could probe further, he began wheezing again, and the tendons in his neck suddenly went taught. His eyes bugged and his face turned an unhealthy shade of purple. He was certainly putting on one hell of a show.  I was about to start drumming my fingers on the leather-topped desk to demonstrate how unimpressed I was and that I was really losing patience, when his body went rigid and he sat bolt upright. His arms were outstretched and the knuckles on his clenched fists ghostly white. Then with a single cough that showered a fine spray of blood onto the surface of the desk, onto the papers in front of him, and onto me, he slumped forward, face down on the desk.

I get up and go round. He's as white as a sheet. I check his neck for a pulse. He's a goner.

'Shit,' I curse under my breath.

It was all I needed. Two missing persons and a dead guy. I'd happily have strangled the little cockcheese myself, but would have preferred to have sapped every last drop of information from him before doing so. Still, it did present me with a golden opportunity to rifle his drawers, his files and his computer's hard-drive. It would save me a break-in later. I gloved up and took my time. It pays to be thorough. There was precious little of interest, but I found a handful of memory sticks that looked like they may contain some interesting details and I was able to copy some records that may or may not come in handy onto an empty stick I had with me. Always be prepared. That's one thing Baden-Powell was right about. He might've been a right-wing pederast, but it does pay to be prepared and to be resourceful.

Once I'd combed the place, I called the pigs. No point doing a runner. I had an appointment, after all: I'd be in the diary at reception and was also, I'd discovered, in Jackson's office diaries, both electronic and paper. It would be rather hard to worm out of the fact I was there. Better to eliminate myself from the investigation right away.

## 5

It took about 15 minutes for them to show. 16 minutes and 53 seconds, to be precise. The ambulance was first on the scene and the paramedics confirmed my diagnosis. I've seen enough corpses in my time to know that no pulse plus not breathing equals dead. Then uniforms flooded the building, just before the plain clothes showed up.

DCI Bradley clocked me straight away. We'd met on a fair few occasions over the years.

'Thunder!' he exclaimed. 'What the fuck are you doing here?'

'You're never gonna believe this, but...' I was straight with him. Told him just as much as he needed to know about my case but didn't mention any of the stuff I'd lifted. Gave him just enough to justify my being there and to establish that I had no motive. Of course, Bradley knew that already. Whether or not he knew I'd have had a quick scout around before his arrival I'm not so sure, but I wasn't about to hand him the ammo and the gun so he could shoot me in the foot. One thing I've learned is that cops aren't generally all that clever. It can be as annoying as hell, but it means that it's not really all that hard to stay one step ahead of them.

'You know I'm going to have to interview you properly and take a formal statement from you, don't you?' he asks in an officious tone. He loves a good suspicious death does Bradley. He might beef about the paperwork, but he fucking loves the rest of the deal. It makes him feel like a proper detective.

I nod as I light another cigarette. 'I know the drill.'

'Good. Walk this way.'

'By the way,' I add as an afterthought, 'this isn't going hit the media, is it?' If the case started getting press attention, it could prove bad, real bad.

'Don't worry. I'll make sure we keep a lid on it.'

The CSIs have turned up and we're ejected from the building as they seal it off. They're certainly not pissing around. Amazing what having money can do for you. Like I say, sex and money. I can guess which one Jackson died for, but will have to do more digging to see if I'm right.

Before we leave, Bradley has a brief exchange with the CSIs and I take the opportunity to peer over the front desk while the receptionists are making their statements. I scan the top page of the open visitor book. The last signatory was a Jacquie Jobson. It rings no bells and I return to Bradley before he has time to notice I've been away.

So go to give my statement to Bradley and his boys. I swear they've got YT kids – or whatever training scheme they have for school dropouts now – filling half the positions on the squad now, because the rozzers seem to be getting younger by the week. Obviously having trouble recruiting. Fear of knife crime and terrorism putting them off, probably. Still, it's a bit of a joke. They'll be employing fucking foetuses on the beat before long.

Once I've given my statement and my time

is my own, I spend the afternoon going through the memory sticks and stuff I lifted, trawling the Internet and making telephone calls. I get through the last of my cigarettes while I'm at it, and resolve – for the third time in as many weeks – to give up. Again. The Internet's certainly taken a lot of the legwork out of this job, and some would probably argue a lot of the skill. I'd probably agree, but you have to move with the times. You can even hire hackers now. I don't exactly approve of such methods myself. There's no substitute for making a stealthy entry to someone's premises under the cover of night and copying all the data you need onto a memory stick or whatever, although it's still not nearly as fun as the old days, rifling through desk drawers and paper files for incriminating evidence. That was proper detective work. It's not that I like getting my hands dirty. I just like to feel any job I do is a job done properly. I guess I'm something of a traditionalist.

It's lazy I know but I decide to check out 118800.co.uk. If I can find any numbers linked to Jackson, it'll be worth giving them a try. He might have phones his wife doesn't know about.

Fucking typical. The mobile phone directory service 118800.co.uk has crashed. The site displays holding page which reads 'service suspended while we make improvements.'

A quick trawl of the news pages tells me all I need to know. Yet again, thousands of users have flocked online to remove their numbers from the site, according to reports. And what a shock: The Twittersphere has been awash with posts from angry users who can't get on the site to make themselves ex-directory, some calling for either Ofcom or the ICO to reappraise the fairness of the service.

I give it up for now. Considering the firm obtained up to 16 million mobile numbers from market research firms as well as online businesses who require customers to leave their contacts details, 118800.co.uk hasn't exactly been the resounding success or revolution it was expected to be. Many campaigners complained of it's being an invasion of privacy, despite UK data protection watchdog the Information Commissioners office having given a green light to the service. Connectivity, the company behind the service, said it only bought customer information which was already in the public domain. Me, I hate the idea, and there's a good reason I use a pay-as-you go mobile and never give my number to anyone, ever. But I have to admit that it has potential to be beneficial in my line of work. If it ever works.

I pull the bottle of J.D. from my desk drawer and pour three fingers of the potent 40% ABV liquor into a tumbler that's sitting on my desk while I consider my next move.

I really ought to change my shirt, but I don't have a spare at the office and don't really have time to go home to pick one up from there. I've got work to do: my pockets are full of memory sticks and shit. A guy's just died in my presence in the most suspicious of circumstances. My case just got a whole lot more complicated and I get the feeling I'm going to have to work fast before things start getting really fucked up. Before I find myself in trouble. Word gets around, and it won't be long before it's known that I witnessed Jackson Jr. breathe his last. So I have to get down to work, and if that's while wearing a shirt with flecks of a dead guy's blood on it, so be it.

Sifting through the reams of dross on Jackson Jr's files, I manage to uncover some contacts that might be worth checking out, see if they know anything. If nothing else, it'll be interesting to find out who they are and what their relationships are with Jackson Jr. I also learn that Jackson Sr. has more than one office and operates under the guise of more than one company. Some are under his own name, others are under various permutations of his pseudonyms. He's clearly one slippery bastard. And he's clearly got plenty to hide. Why else would he work under so many guises and run so many different companies rather than trade under one single umbrella? Jackson Jr's argument that it spreads risk is fair enough but it only goes so far and doesn't explain the different names. Ok, so I have a suspicious mind, but it means I'm better than most at spotting suspicious activities. And suspicious characters. Jackson just screams suspicious to me. And how he's missing. Which is pretty damn suspicious.

While perusing Jackson's files, I'm keeping one eye on the various news feeds to see if anyone's reporting his disappearance. So far, so good. The last thing I want is heat and journos and paps staking out every location on my list of places to check out. It's a pretty slow day for news. Besides, can you imagine the media frenzy that would kick off if word got out that Michael Jackson was missing? Even if it wasn't the one that's a multi-billion dollar industry, a recording artist and a paedophile. The fact that he snuffed it doesn't seem to have registered with some people. A lot of people, in fact. Conspiracy theories surrounding his death have raged from within hours of the news breaking and there's been no abatement since. There's more speculation over this single event than Diana, Roswell and the fucking moon landing in combination. But that's nothing compared to the number of people who speculate that he might still be alive. Worse still, those who insist that he *is* still alive. Those who can't believe he's dead and wake up bawling and spend hours a day moping at their home-made shrines like he's some deity. It's insanity. So even now, a headline about a missing 'Michael Jackson' would be likely to go global in seconds because of all of the idiots. And it would make my job really fucking difficult, I'm sure of that.

On the feed, another item about some pervert, billed as a 'sick' 'sexual predator,' the media and the press wheeling out the tired old clichés again. This popular phraseology concerns me, the association with sexual predation with being 'sick' or 'perverted.' Doesn't all sexual interaction contain a predatory aspect? In the first instance, the courtship is a waggledance that involves the hunting, 'the thrill of the chase' – a practice ritualised, glorified, in chivalric and renaissance literature, poetry, society, the Elizabethan and Henrician court, generally considered a 'romantic' ideal in today's society.

I'm finding it particularly difficult to concentrate: there's a lot playing on my mind, a lot of information that I simply can't piece together. It's early days for this case, but I usually like to start with an angle or a hunch. I'm getting a tingle, but nothing I can really put my finger on. Perhaps it's just nicotine cravings. I've not had a smoke in a three hours and 12 minutes. I need to get to a newsagents. And of course, a laundrette.

First things first. I have to check out all of Jackson's offices. One isn't much of an office, so much as a lock-up on the outskirts of town. I'm going to need a car, so I have to move quickly to get myself to a rental place before it closes. I can use the cash I got for the deposit and charge the car to expenses. There's no way I can get there by bus and I'm sure as hell not taking a taxi. And it has to be tonight. So I take a bus out to the car hire place – Budget. I never take the piss with expenses.

I fancied the Mercedes C180 1.8 but opted for the cheaper and less conspicuous 5-door Ford Focus 1.6 TDCI. The engine was keen, and while the quiet engine is marred by a lot of road noise, the sports suspension makes for a firm ride. And with $CO_2$ emissions of just $114 - 125g/km$, I feel less guilt cruising in a Focus than in many other cars.

According to Jackson Jr.'s diary, both he and Jackson Sr. are due to meet with a Ben Blakemore at 19:00. Blakemore's going to be in for a surprise. Assuming he shows, that is. As I said, word gets around. He might already be wise to the fact Jackson Jr.'s dead, and he's bound to know that

Jackson Sr.'s missing by now. But I need to check out the office and I need to check out Blakemore, so it makes sense to kill two birds with one stone, and it's generally better to catch marks off their guard. They're more likely to spill when they're surprised.

## 6

I extinguish my cigarette with the sole of my shoe and roll on up to the guy. In truth, he's nothing but a kid in a suit. He's taller than me, 6'1" but weedy, no more than 10 stone and about 22. And as cocky as fuck. I'd left the car in the next street and taken the last few hundred yards on foot. It might mean running to make it back to the vehicle later, but it's always a good idea to put some distance between yourself and your transport because you never know who's watching. He clocked me from a fair distance, and if that hadn't been enough to blow my intended element of surprise, the fact he recognised me really did draw the heat out of my sting.

'Evenin',' he calls out as I approach. As I said, cocky as fuck. So he knew who I was, and also knew I had nothing on him. It might take some serious bluffing to wring anything of use out of this sharp-dressed smart-arse.

'Bill Thunder,' I say, offering my hand while I struggle to place him. He looks familiar alright, but I don't know a Ben Blakemore. I always remember a name. Besides, I'd had a scan of my files and hadn't found any mention of him, and I'm nothing if not thorough.

'Ben Blakemore,' he beams, wrapping his long bony fingers around mine and making a concerted effort to crush them with 60lbs psi grip, pumping my arm five times in rapid succession. The smile's superficially friendly, but is as fake as his

Rolex and the eyes are glazed. I can spot a bullshitter.

'Good to see you again.' I have no qualms flipping pleasantries out to smarms like Blakemore. They see it as a sign we're on the same footing or something. Makes me laugh to see bluffers who can't spot bluffers, especially when they know they're bluffing and being bluffed. And I wasn't going to let on that I had no recollection of having met him before

'Likewise. I'm guessing you're not here on a pleasant stroll that's detoured by this way. You're looking for Jackson.' He smiles. Freshmint. I can always smell a bullshitter too. Gum's invariably covering something.

I grunt.

'Either, both?'

'Well, Jackson the elder's missing, as we both well know,' I say. 'And Jr.'s unlikely to show now, unless someone stretchers him from the morgue especially for this meeting.'

His features cloud.

'Are you saying he's dead?'

'As a dodo.'

His expression and tone are, I believe, of genuine surprise. Probably the first genuine feelings he's felt in years. This guy's no more a high-flyer than I am, and my instincts tell me he's not exactly criminal so much as a chancer, a bullshit artist, and a wheeler-dealer type. Associating with the Jacksons is likely to be a real step up for this small-timer.

'Ah.'

'Indeed.'

'So, how can I help?' The smile returns. He can't help himself, the charm tap always works its way to the on position with him.

'Well, you can tell me how you know Jackson.'

'Mr. Jackson called me and said he had some work for me. Asked me to meet him here.'

'He called you?'

'Yes,' he nods like an eager puppy with a stick being waved in front of its nose.

'When was that?'

'Yesterday.'

'When?'

'Afternoon. Around 4.'

'And did he say what the work was?' I press.

He shakes his head. 'Wouldn't say. Just said it would pay well and to meet him here.'

'You didn't think this was an odd place to meet a high-profile businessman?' I quiz.

'I suppose,' he concedes, 'but I didn't really question it. I needed the work and if he said it would pay well, I believed him.'

'Fair enough. Done any work for him before?'

'No.'

'And how d'you know him?'

'I don't really. Friend of an acquaintance, I suppose.' I hated it when people talked vague like that. Trying to sound well-connected without giving anything away. Usually bullshit and easy to make the connections.

'That mutual friend being Reynolds?'

He nods. 'Yes.'

'I understand you spoke to Reynolds the night before he disappeared.'

The grin's still here but the eyes darken. 'Where'd you hear that?'

He's playing tough. I can play tough back. 'Got my sources. It's my job.'

'Might've done. What's it to you?'

If there's one thing worse than someone playing it cool and withholding information, it's someone who doesn't know Jack pretending they know something while playing it cool and withholding information they don't got.

'Nothing to me. No skin off my nose. But any information that leads me to Reynolds might get him out of a tough spot. And it's not just Reynolds. There's a lot hanging on the discovery of his whereabouts. Lives depending on it, you catch my drift.' I'm playing it up, while being intentionally vague.

'What's in it for me?'

'Not getting your arse whipped.' I shoot back. The tosser's trying my patience now.

He looks at me. We lock eyes. He tries to stare me out, but doesn't last long. He knows I'm not fucking about. He visibly deflates. His shoulders slump, his head drops, his eyes fall to his shiny leather shoes.

'I saw him. It was with a group of people at lunch. We were in The Exchequer. He got a call and said he had to go and he left in a hurry. Looked serious. I didn't get to talk to him.'

'Did you get any indication of where he might've been going?'

'No. I was talking to someone else and wasn't really paying attention, y'know?'

'Yeah. Any idea who might've been calling him?'

'No.'

'Ok. Cheers, you've been a big help.'

'Really?'

'No.'

Time for a change of tack. He won't stay tight-lipped for long. With a deft swivel of my pelvis, I raise my knee. My bony knee-cap connects firmly with both his scrotum and his perineum. Double whammy: bingo! The tosser bends double in agony, tears of pain surging to eyes and running down his flushed face.

'What the fuck?' he gasps.

'Look, Cook, I don't know what's with the Ben Blakemore shit but I know who you are and I know you're a snivelling little shit with his tongue up the arse of every wannabe gangster in this city.' Yes, I'd figured out how I recognised him now. Tommy Cook was a waste of space, all mouth and no action, as likely to bite the hand that fed him if he thought he might make some personal gain, however small. Renowned as a rat, too. A gangly chain-wearing, tracksuit-sporting small-time drug-dealing B-boy until a few years ago – which earned him the nickname Tom Westwood, as much on account of his complete lack of credibility as for his image – he was nothing, nada, zero, zip, zilch. What the fuck Jackson was doing with this no-hoper I couldn't begin to guess, at least not now. 'I believe you're completely clueless as to what's going on with the Jacksons, but I don't for a second believe you don't know shit about Reynolds' activities.'

'I s-swear,' he stammered.

Another knee to the nads and he doubles over again. He looks up at me, eyes bugging, almost exophthalmic. I'd have happily taken him apart, but some restraint was appropriate under the circumstances.

'Try to be a big boy, and end up just a kid,' I snarled. 'You might be hanging out with Reynolds and almost have got to do errands for the Jacksons, but you're the smallest of the small-fry, a wannabe.'

'Fuck you,' he spat, but I could tell he was about to buckle. He swung at me, and although I dodged the centre of his fist, the blow still glanced my cheekbone.

Neurons flashed as my pain receptors sent signals surging round my nervous system. I was riled now. In a reflex retaliation, I dealt him a swift blow in the stomach. He deflated like a punctured balloon. Stale breath tinged with Freshmint vacated his feeble lungs.

'Now talk,' I snapped, standing over him as he sat, curled into a ball on the asphalt.

And the little runt squealed like a piggy. I got what I came for. Wasn't much, but it was a start. I'd wrung all I was going to get out of Cook the Crook. He was bottom of the food-chain, after all. I still dealt him another blow to the genitals as a parting shot, however. Don't want scums like that breeding. The world's got more pond-life than it needs already.

## 7

Time to call in a favour. I rang Gash and we arranged to meet, bringing our pre-arranged drinks forward a few days. This wasn't going to be a social appointment. It was business: I needed him on the team on this. His contacts were exactly what I needed. Pooling resources made sense, and I'd be happy to split the pay if it meant cracking the case. Not that I'd need him for everything: I'd got myself a couple of half-decent leads from that little wanker Cook the Crook, and a few more from Jackson Jr.'s files. So I'd be offering him a 25% cut. It was more than generous, as I'd only be asking him to do 10% to 15% of the work, maximum. Besides, having Roger on the case would be something of a risk. It was always a gamble with Gash. He was a shit-hot dick, but he had a knack of being something of a liability at times. A bit of a lose cannon.

First pint down and Roger's giving me the low-down on his recent inquiries, which confirm that our current investigations converge, but for now I keep that to myself and leave the talking to him. He's a great talker.

'So I swing by to have a chat with Reynolds' girl. "I'd rather jack! I ain't telling you shit," she tells me, so I put the squeeze on her some, hoping she'll squeal. No such luck, so in the end I have to resort to putting my special move on her.'

I groan. I know the move. It's legendary. I taught him it. The plagiarist.

'Why are you such a brutal misogynist bastard?' I ask him. I'm half kidding.

'I'm no common or garden misogynist!' he snorts, rolling his eyes. He loves this shit, and I can predict the punchline. 'I'm a misanthrope of galactic proportion!' he bombasts. Oh yeah.

I know I shouldn't ask, but can't help myself. 'What choice of instrument?'

'Longarm stapler,' he bugles.

I wince. 'Brutal.'

'Effective,' Rog nods. 'And resourceful. She was working in an office. And it's important to send out the right kind of message.'

'Which is?'

'Don't fuck with Gash.'

'As if.....' Kind of like an 'amen.' I know the guy well enough not to fuck with him, and he's on my side. I light a cigarette.

'Didn't know you'd started smoking again,' he observes, raising an eyebrow.

'I haven't, I deadpan. 'I'm just practising for when I do.'

'Another?' he raises his empty glass.

'Hell yeah.'

Roger heads to the bar and I survey the scene. Smoke hangs thick as voices rise and drift through the air. Bare oak beams support the wooden ceiling: the bar has the appearance, at least internally, of a barn, or an ancient aircraft hangar. Bare wooden floorboards are dirty, unvarnished, splintering, stained and sticky with ale spillage, phlegm, piss and vomit. Ash, cigarette butts and broken glass litter the boards, along with discarded crisp packets match boxes and spent rubbers. Roger's choice of venue. Sometimes I think he enjoys being pissed off and uncomfortable.

At the far end of the room, there's a long, mess-style wooden table on nailed-in trestles, long wooden benches running parallel up either length of the table jammed with student types. I zone into their conversation. It's a curse. I can't help myself: I'm a compulsive reader – signs, newspapers over shoulders, whatever – and a compulsive eavesdropper.

'Oasis. Yeah, love 'em. Rockin',' one average youth is saying loudly.

'Yeah. An' the Beatles, right,' adds another guy in faded, baggy-cut blue denims, Nike trainers and an anorak.

'I reckon the Stone Roses really 'ad summink, y'know?' comes the contribution from another.

These cunts don't know shit.

I turn my attention to a guy at the end of the table. He is wearing a jelly-mould sun-hat pulled low, so as to partially obscure his eyes. The geezer has hair – masses and masses of unkempt, unwashed, bushy, dark, wavy hair. His monster sideburns are low-slung, meeting his fuzzed jawbone. They are bushy, frizzing out over his ears, encroaching over his cheeks in a lamb-chop figure. Where he has no sideburn, four days worth of dark, dense stubble covers his face. His hair reaches his shoulders and covers his anorak's collar and the huge wings of his shirt collars. The 30" flares say

'70s throwback copyist retro motherfucker'. He stares straight ahead as if seeing beyond the precipice of humanity and into void and in a deep Mancunian monotone simply issues forth a single word:

'Man.'

All the children seated around the table look to one another in fleeting bewilderment before resuming their fragmented conversations, ignoring the hairy freak. I almost feel sorry for the guy, albeit fleetingly. He's clearly the only one with any sense of music history, and it's a pity he's such an inarticulate cretin and completely devoid of style or originality.

It's not that I claim originality. I'm a cliché and I know it. But then, I'm a dick and I'm the epitome of hard-boiled. It's not my job to be original. It's my job to find shit out and occasionally fuck shit up. After all, I'm the Bastardizer.

Back over to where I'm seated and Roger's back with a pint and a J.D. I can tell by his expression that he's not about to break into some regular barroom beer and football ramble. He resumes his seat opposite me and leans in, a serious expression on his face. He takes a large slug from his J.D. over ice. He is tall. Very tall, and lean. His hair is tufty and unkempt and on his chin is a metaller's goatee tuft. His sharp features bear a very earnest expression, and his spindly metaller's moustache twitches occasionally as he emphasizes each point with the utmost of care and deliberation.

'I think there are two modes of plagiarism

which are acceptable…' he begins.

'…even if not wholly legitimate,' I interject by way of concluding the point.

'Needless to say,' he continues with a nod of arrogance, 'plagiarism and legitimacy aren't really in the same field. That's not my point here, as I think you well know. But what I am saying is that it's okay to plagiarise under certain circumstances, of which there are two:

'Either you're so sneaky about what you're nicking that it just doesn't ever get noticed by anyone ever, which is pretty damn cool, or you're so blatant with it, acknowledging sources all over the place, so that people actually get in on it and play with the piece, consciously looking all the time, combing through, to see if they can tell what's been lifted and from where.'

'Indeed… Elastica were masters of the latter mode in music,' I volunteer. 'Things are rather different now, though. Both in music and literature.'

The bar may well have been the seediest dive in this town, overpopulated by students and other miscellaneous dosser types, but the clientele provided him with a constant source of inspiration and light relief. When assignments were few, Roger would concentrate his efforts on writing. As yet unpublished, he believed he had what it takes. Yes, the literary world really did need more hard-boiled detective fiction, and he was ready to prove it. Dashiel Hammett? Raymond Chandler? Mickey Spillane? Step aside, here's Roger Gash…

Gash nodded.

'Maybe you're right,' I conceded as I sank my pint in one. I sat and glanced about the smoggy bar. 'So…' I lit a cigarette and drew hard. The tip glowed red and the paper receded toward his mouth. Smoke rose from the growing length of ash and spilled from my mouth as he spoke. Yes, I had caved.

'So, the smoking?' Gash pedalled.

'Yeah. As of about three hours ago.' I rolled my eyes. I felt a bit of a prick, succumbing after one close call like the one with Cook, when I even had the situation fully under control. But I couldn't help but worry there'd be repercussions.

'Hey, it's cool,' he said, lighting up another for himself.

I changed the subject. After all, we'd not touched for a single second on business yet. 'So, not much been doing down at the office, eh?'

Roger wasn't listening. Instead, he was casting a baleful eye over the students in the corner.

'Students,' he spat with heavy disdain.

'Mmm?'

'I hate fucking students.'

'Don't fuck students then. You're getting too old for that anyway.'

'Funny twat.'

'Guilty.'

'I'm serious though. I hate them. All of them. The thing is, you can hate tem collectively, because they're not individuals, and they're all so fucking smug. And what have they got to be smug about? *Oh, I'm SOOO stressed! I've got 500 words to write by next month.*' And then they finish up and go and temp as data inputters. What the hell have they got to be so fucking smug about? Nothing! I mean, look at that fuckwit in the corner.'

'Sunhat dude?'

'Yeah. I mean, I like living in a culturally diverse society, I really do, blah, blah, blah, and all that, but how can he be there in his sunhat and flares and be so smug about everything? I mean, he actually thinks he's cool looking like that. And he thinks he's, like, original or something. And his body language tells me that he's smug about that...I mean, for fuck's sake...!'

I nodded. Roger had to have his obligatory rant about students. Not that I actually minded. I'm hardly the biggest fan of the student stereotype myself. But when Roger started his anti-student tirade...well, you just had to let him go. He was draining the remaining Jack Daniel's from the glass and pulling a 'sour' face. He was tall. He was lean. He was Roger Gash. He was hard-boiled. He was THE hard-boiled dick.

I zone out momentarily and return to my senses to find Roger in full rant again.

'...and he's so smug looking! Up himself? I can't see his fucking torso!'

'So anything much doing at the office?'

'A bit, Bill, a bit,' replies Roger.
'Do tell.'
'Well, first off, did I tell you they'd busted the 2D Kid?'
'No...' I'm assuming this is different from the 2D Kid I met yesterday.

'Yeah. Hauled his ass in yesterday. Turned out it was all a front.'

'No shit?'

'Nope. Absolutely no fucking shit. Straight up.'

'Christ.'

'Not Jackson, I take it?'

'Jackson? Oh, hell, no. No, no. Sorry. I forgot we had a 2D Kid closer to home. I heard he got deep sixed yesterday.'

'You heard right. One of the reasons I wanted to see you, as it happens.'

'Really? Ok. Well come back to that, 'cause this is a fucking bitching piece of shit... today... yeah, woah, we had some pretty fucking hardcore torture going down in the Shit Street lockups. Some mean-assed motherfucker with a grudge against some dude who dicked his bitch... Get this: the dude who's chick had been doin' the cheatin' tattooed a life-size manta ray into his rival's chest using a blunt razorblade. He incorporated the nipples to be the eyes, right, and he did this tattoo before removing the nipples with a pair of garden sheers. While he was still in shock over the tattooing and loss of both nipples, 'capped him with a crowbar. 'Cause, then he couldn't move, 'cause his hands were tied and his kneecaps out, so he was unable to defend himself against having a cheese grater applied to his scrotum and his penis sliced in two lengthways like a banana split with a machete...' Gash got strangely animated whenever he relayed tales of the utmost brutality. If I didn't know better I'd think he got a buzz off it.

'Fuck, that's brutal.'

'Yeah. Guy passed out. Brought him to with a monster shot of adrenaline before they finished him off - get this - by being disemboweled with a chainsaw...then they dismembered the corpse with a Stanley knife and pinned 2" square chunks of diced flesh to every wanted poster for the Harlem Hardnut in 3 states.'

It was always the way. We spent 90% of our time digressing and exchanging brutalities, and even forgot completely to talk business at times. And Roger operated on both sides of the Atlantic. It sometimes seems as though he forgot which side he was on when he delivered his anecdotes.

'No shit?'

'No shit. Straight up.'

'Shit.'

'No.'

Drinks flowed, but I managed to steer the conversation in the direction I was aiming. Roger was a loose cannon and no mistake. But I liked the guy. His intelligence was often astounding and he never ceased to surprise me in one way or another.

So, he was on board, and had some files and contacts I might find of use. He'd email them over the following morning. He also said he would do some digging, talk to some people. He had contacts all over. However wayward he was, Roger could be relied on to deliver the goods. I stumbled home at kicking out time. I was going to feel less than great in the morning. I'd regret that. After all, I had work to do.

## 8

Sure enough, when the alarm went at the usual time I awoke feeling like shit. I lugged myself out of bed, the usual drill. I got my last clean dirty shirt out of the wardrobe, dressed and hauled myself to the office, smoking a cigarette and calling in for my morning coffee en route. The three-day downpour had stopped and it was now full summer heat again. 16.5°C, and only 7:30 in the morning. It was going to be a roaster and no mistake.

One thing that I'd learned from Jackson Jr.'s files was that Jackson Sr. had not only multiple offices, but also a summerhouse he took off to with Mrs. Jackson for long weekends. I'd been thinking of ringing her to ask if she'd checked it out since his disappearance when the phone rang.

'W. T. P. D. A.'
'Hello…' a familiar female voice.
'Thunder's?'
'Yes.'
'Mr Thunder?'
'Yes.' Get to the point...
'Jacinta Jackson.'
'Hello, Mrs. Jackson,' I smooth. I feel anything but. My head's pounding and my tongue is rasping against my teeth. I want to die. 'How can I help you today?'
'I just wanted to see how things were going,' she says. She sounds agitated. Or perhaps it's

just that I'm projecting my hangover and my anxiety onto her.

'Slow.' There's no point in bullshitting her. 'I've enlisted an assistant, but that'll be counted in with the standard fee. No extra charge.' I tell her. 'But I've had to hire a car.'

'You did mention...'

'Ah, yes. Well, just so you know, it's not for idle pissing about. I had to take it to the outskirts of town last night to follow up on a lead. And I'm about to head out to the summerhouse you and Mr. Jackson keep.'

I could hear her breathing change. It was subtle, but I'm as sharp as a razor. Even with a hangover from hell. Something about the summerhouse hit a nerve or something. This piqued my interest. I knew better than to push it now. There were other ways of finding out.

A meet-up would perhaps be a good start. The lubrication of a drink or two ought, in theory, to loosen off some of the armour, and then it's in for the kill: hack, hack, hack. A neat slice from the midriff to the solar plexus. Part the dermal curtains of social front and then begin the operation, routing to the heart of the matter. Cut the fat, split the ribcage, separate out the component parts. Haul out those entrails, give those vital organs the close inspection they so deserve. Part spleen from sinew, colon from intestine... severance of blood and bone, muscle and matter, see it all stretched out. Watch her spill. That was the intention. It was not borne out of cruelty, merely a thirst for knowledge. Then I would know.

I put it to her that we should meet and she agrees. Apparently she had some information she didn't want to divulge over the telephone anyway. Score! She suggested some ghastly wine-bar slap-bang in the city centre at 15:00 and I agreed because it doesn't do to piss a client off, especially not a hot one who's willing to stump up the ackers for a missing husband. So I could endure a spot of discomfort for an hour or so.

Between the call and the designated meet time, I flip through more of Jackson Jr.'s emails. Some would accuse me of being a nosey cunt, but me, I prefer to call it thoroughness. Leave no stone unturned, no email or file unread. You never know. Ok, so I didn't find anything of interest, but hey. As I say, you never know.

I arrived in Yates's at 14:58:22, headed straight for the bar and ordered myself a straight J.D., no ice, no Coke. There's no beer. Thankfully, the place is quiet. These trendy chains invariably attract the kind of people I despise. The barbint looks perplexed, like she's never served a neat spirit before. As she stretches up to draw the shot from the optic, I wince at the sight of her broad, flabby ass in her tight skirt that stops mid-thigh. Thighs like fucking tree-trunks, too. But then, her upper arms are comparable to my thighs. A teenager, overfed and spoiled rotten by her parents, driven everywhere in the 4x4, she walks like a spastic. She lollops over with my drink. I hand her a £5 note and receive less change than I would have hoped.

Moments later, before I had time to move from the bar, Mrs. Jackson appears at my side.

'Mr. Thunder,' she acknowledges.

'Call me Bill,' I tell her, raising my glass.

She orders a Pinot Grigiot for herself and a J.D. She's obviously a keen observer. Either that or she's making assumptions and has got me pegged as the cliché I am. She gesticulates toward the spirit as she lifts the wine glass to her lips. Condensation is already forming and beginning to run to the stem.

'Bill,' she says, running her ringer round the rim of her glass. I can't tell if she's being coquettish or nervous. Perhaps both. 'I've found a few things I think you should see.'

'Uh-huh,' I nod, encouraging her to go on.

'Papers,' she says, glancing round anxiously.

'Are you ok?' I ask her straight.

'Not really,' she confirms. 'I feel like I'm being watched. It's making me nervous.'

'Hell, you're making me nervous,' I chuckle in an attempt to lighten the mood. It doesn't work.

'I can't help it,' she says, taking a large swig of wine.

'Why don't you tell me about it,' I suggest.

'I've moved to a hotel for a while,' she says, her breath a little shaky.

'Really? Why's that?'

'I don't feel entirely safe at home,' she intimates.

'Being alone?'

'It's more than that.' She looks at me. 'Mister... Bill? I need protection.'

'There's only so much I can do,' I remind her.

'A car followed me home from work the other night.' She's serious.

I prick up my ears. 'Are you sure?'

'Yes. I'm not just being paranoid. It tailed me, a few cars behind all the way. I even took a detour, completely out of the way. There's no way anyone would take that route to get to my street. Then it pulled up a few doors up from the house and stayed there. It had blacked-out windows, and no-one got out. No one got in, either. It just sat there.'

'Hmm. Did you get a look at the plates?'

'I'm sorry. I didn't think. I was too shaken up.'

'And I'm guessing you didn't notice the make or model?'

She looked pained and shook her head.

'I'm a complete girl when it comes to cars. It was

66

black. 4x4. Like a Land Rover. Or a Subaru or something?' the inflection in her voice signaled her uncertainty. But she was perhaps less of a girl or more observant, than she knew, or was letting on. Something clicked.

'Hmm.' I jotted this snippet down in the pad I kept in my pocket.

'A Subaru, you say?'

'Yes. Is that what I mean? You know, one of those... I'm not sure how you pronounce it.'

'Yeah, Subaru,' I confirm.

'But I'm not certain, y'know? Just something like that. But it was definitely black, with blacked out windows.'

I'd seen a black Subaru Forester SUV parked over the road from the offices of Jackson and Co. shortly before I'd witnessed the dying breaths of the head honcho. Ok, so these vehicles are pretty commonplace, but the 2.5 XTEn in Obsidian Black Pearl, which comes with 17" alloy wheels and boasts a 230 PS Turbocharged engine capable of acceleration from 0-62 mph in just 7.6 seconds, is pretty distinctive. Besides, I don't believe in coincidence.

'It's a start,' I tell her.

'Or it might have been a Jeep.' She looks flustered.

'Don't worry,' I assure her. 'Had you seen it before?'

'Possibly, but again, I can't be sure. I think I saw it outside my office, maybe once or twice.'

'When was that?'

'Just before Michael left on his trip,' she says, her lip trembling slightly.

'Hmm.'

'And then there was a man outside the house last night. In the back garden.'

'Really?' I prick up my ears.

'Yes.'

'Did you get a decent look at him? Enough to give any kind of description?' I press.

'No,' she sighs. 'It was dark. He was dressed in black. All over. Black jumper, wool hat. Looked like sniper or something. Like in films. I was going through from the living room into the kitchen. I put the light on and there he was, at the window. I screamed and he disappeared. I was terrified. I didn't think to look out of the window until it was too late and he'd gone. And I was too scared to go and look in the garden. I just went round and made sure all the doors and windows were locked – good job I did, too, because the window to Mark's office was ajar and I was sure I'd closed it. Must be all that's going on, making me forgetful.'

'There was no sign of anyone having been inside?' I query.

'Not that I can tell. But then, I don't really

go in there all that much. It's his space. I keep out of it, you know? He likes his privacy, and he likes to keep things... well, not tidy, really, but, in a certain way, y'know?'

'Yeah. A guy and his office. It's not something you want to interfere with. There's a reason I've stayed single.' Maybe I'm giving too much away.

'I get the impression you're a petty singular kinda guy,' Jacinta said, a vague smile curling her full, crimson lips. 'And that you're probably married to your job.'

'Well, yeah, I suppose that's pretty much the measure of it,' I concede. 'I do take time off occasionally, though,' I added as something of an afterthought.

'I'm glad to hear it,' she said, draining her glass and looking at me, fluttering her long mascara'd lashes.

I remind myself what I'm here for. I'm on business. I needed information, and as she kept pulling back the moment it looked as though something really useful might be forthcoming, I was going to have to stick with the original plan. 'Refill?'

'Mmm, please. The same again. Pinot Grigiot. A large one.'

'You got it.'

There was no-one waiting at the bar and so I got served quickly. I had to be careful, I didn't want to put away too many myself. While I can hold my drink, I needed to stay sharp. Plus I had to drive later. But in order to do so, I needed more information about the Jackson's summerhouse. What I'd got so far – a Subaru and a surveillance operation of sorts – was good, but I needed more. Much more. I got the feeling that Mrs. Jackson was holding out on me. It was bugging me. The real problem was that I couldn't see why she'd withhold potentially valuable information. She way paying me to help her, after all. Wasn't she?

'So, about the summerhouse...' I begin as I put her drink in front of her. Time for a more direct approach. Well, she is on her third now.

'Yes? Oh, yes...' she looks a little confused. 'Oh, yes, I had to tell you something. The reason I called you.'

'Yes?' I'd almost forgotten that she'd called me with the promise of information. Perhaps I was misreading her. Perhaps she was simply struggling to remain focused what with all that was going on. Her husband was missing, after all. And Jackson Jr. had also died only yesterday. She didn't seem all that cut up about it, though, if I was being truly objective and cynical.

'I'm sorry, I get distracted,' she says casting her eyes downward and focusing her gaze in the rings from the base of her glass that were mapped out on the table top like the remains of iron-age hut circles on the hillside when viewed from an aerial perspective. 'I'm finding it all rather difficult right now.'

'Don't worry. I understand.'

'Look, anyway, so the thing is I found these papers in Mark's office. I wasn't snooping or prying, I just... well, they were under a few bits in his drawers. And I had a quick look through them and was pretty shocked. I mean, I had no idea. I wanted you to see them.'

'Ok. You have them with you?'

'God. No. They're at the hotel. In my safe. I didn't want to bring them out with me.'

'Right.' I paused. 'Look, I don't understand why you don't call the police,' I said sternly. 'I mean, I'm a PI. I'm a bit of a sucker for the damsel in distress deal, but protection's not in my remit. I've got enough people out for me as it is. Besides, if you've got people after you, it's a police matter. Either that, or it's personal. Whichever, it's not my job to put my neck on the line, you know what I mean?'

She nods, looks crestfallen. 'I know it's not your responsibility,' she says, a tear coming to her eye.

## 9

We finished up our drinks and caught a cab to the hotel she was staying at. It was one of those big chain ones, an Ibis: 800 hotels in 40 countries around the world. I was quite surprised by this. I'd thought she might've gone a bit more upmarket, but the size of the suite made up for the generic nature of the accommodation. It was pretty fucking huge.

She fixed us both drinks then went to the safe. She removed a manila foolscap envelope which she handed to me before sitting on the sofa. She kicked off her expensive-looking shoes – a different pair from the other day – before crossing her shapely legs. Her skirt was shorter – mid thigh – and rode up a little as she did so. I needed to focus and instead of looking at her as she kicked back and unfastened a button or two on her blouse – it was fucking baking in there, 27°C and not a degree lower – I slipped the contents from the envelope. A few pieces of correspondence, a couple of bank statements and a certified copy of Mark's will. It was dated three days before he left on the business trip from which he had failed to return.

'These?' I ask, hoping for a pointer.

'Yes. That in particular.' She's meaning the will.

It doesn't take long for the penny to drop. She isn't named on it. Everything goes to Jackson

Jr. and of course, that's how she and Jackson Jr. can be about the same age: she isn't his mother. In no time at all, Jacinta's unraveled much of the Jackson history I need to make sense of things. Jackson Jr. is his son from his first marriage. Jacinta is in fact Mrs. Jackson III.

'But you do realize that this would make you the prime suspect for the murder of Jackson Jr.? if he's without an heir...'

'Of course. *That's* why I've not gone to the police with any of this.'

I feel like a complete prick. I'm supposed to be a detective. 'Figures now,' I grunt. In my defense, this information wasn't readily available, and I was only a few days into a case that was pretty complex and had taken a turn for the nasty only a day in. 'So, the summerhouse?' I stern up. It's hard to concentrate with that much leg and cleavage on display, and she doesn't appear to be wearing a bra either. Must keep my composure.

She fixes herself another drink: I decline this time. My glass is still half-full anyway. Or half-empty, depending on how you look at it. She really is sinking them. Resuming her position on the couch she gives me details of its location and tells me how she got nervous last time she and Jackson stayed there after some shady looking guys called by and Jackson disappeared for over an hour to 'talk' with them. It had been about three months ago. She'd not been back since – Jackson had been too busy and she'd been too scared, although she used to take herself off for quiet weekends before that to read magazines and generally have some peaceful Jacinta time away from work and everything else. She'd not got a proper look at them or their vehicle, but she thought it might've been an SUV.

'Like the Subaru or whatever it was?'

She pondered a moment. 'Yeah. Now you mention it. I'd not made the connection.'

'That's why I'm the detective,' I winked. I can be a smooth fucker at times.

'Bill,' she said, looking down, 'I'm scared. And lonely.'

'We all are,' I grimaced.

'Please...' She gently patted the space beside her on the sofa.

I did as she bid. Immediately she inched closer until she was pressing against me. She looked up at me, her full, crimson lips pouting. She had curves in all the right places, and would've been hard for any red-blooded male to resist at that moment. She rested her head on my shoulder. Before I knew it, those full, crimson lips were pressed against mine. She snaked her tongue between my lips and kissed me hard. I may not be so young, but I'm still ruggedly handsome. I figure she must be ten or twelve years my junior. Not bad work if you can get it. And she's paying me! Sex and money, sex and money...

I can feel her heat and her perfume is subtle but nevertheless overwhelming as it weaves its way up my nostrils and to my scent receptors.

Her pheromones flood my olfactory canals and I'm no longer my own master. Moments later her blouse is on the floor and one of her stiff nipples is between my upper and lower central incisors. She hitches her skirt – stockings, not tights – and I penetrate her dripping gash with my throbbing member, the erectile tissue engorged with hot blood. My glans rubs against her cervix in a flood of her vaginal lubricant and she grips my shaft with her swollen blood-filled vulva. I ejaculate hard, shooting my 10cc – and then some – of hot seminal fluid, and she's riding a wave of orgasms far from quietly.

We lie on the king-size bed, panting, perspiration glistening on our naked bodies. We do not speak. I check my watch. Quick, clean and efficient. I gotta go.

'Bill...' she says imploringly.

'Sorry, I have to go. Work to do.'

## 10

I've got a good couple of hours or so before I have to leave, so get myself back to the office, stopping by at a 24-hour off-license for cigarettes on the way. I call by my regular independent coffee house that stays open later than most for a strong tall Americano. Black, five sugars. It can't be the three or four drinks I've consumed that are making me feel a little strange, but I'm hoping the caffeine injection will straighten me out a bit and help restore me to my usual self. I hate not feeling entirely right. I can still smell Jacinta's perfume and as I catch sight of my reflection in a shop window en route to my office I notice I've got her lipstick on my collar. Shit. Good job I'm single. It's not a good look, but at least tonight's operation will be solitary and under the cover of darkness. No-one will notice. Maybe I should start wearing darker shirts. I'm getting sick of stainey shirts and looking like a tramp, especially when I'm busy. Laundry really isn't high in my priorities, but I'm going to have to do some soon.

There were new messages on the answerphone. It wasn't unusual, They'd be either threats or wrong numbers, probably. I get a lot of both.

'Hello? Is that Pizza Express? I was looking to book a table for tonight. I've been calling for ages and no-one's picking up. Are you open? I'll try again later but if you get this message, can you call me? I need to book as soon as possible. Party of five. My number is 07887 482326.' Bozo. Sadly, far from unique. My number's nothing like Pizza Express' either.

'I know where you live... I know where you're hidin.' You can be out now, you can ignore the phone, and you can give me the slip for now but I'll find you. I'm gonna hunt you down and cut you into little pieces, you hear?' I hear. Idle threats, idle threats. You get to tell the difference between the ones that mean business and the ones that are just trying to put the wind up after hearing enough – and finding out the hard way which ones follow through. There are some you ignore at your peril. This, I was confident, was just so much hot air. Not least of all because this same guy had been leaving calls off and on for months now and never done a thing. The world's fill of cranks, and I've managed to attract more than my share through the years. I deleted it.

'Bill, Roger here, I'm on the case. Gonna do some digging. I'll be going to ground for a few days. You know the drill. I'll be in touch, say, a week. Stay low, and watch your back.' Typical Gash. Credit where he's due, he usually surfaced with something worthwhile after going under for a few days. I don't know how he does it, but he does. Gash delivers the goods, and I'm glad to have him aboard.

'Hey. I don't know who the fuck you think you are, but I'm onto you. Yes, I am.' Another male voice. This one sounded angry, and didn't want to be recognised. The vocal was distorted, and, by the sound of it, pitch shifted. 'You better stay well away.

Keep your filthy fuckin' hands off my girl and stay well the fuck out of my business. I know what you're doing. And I saw you in the bar and at the hotel today. You're playin' with fire. You better fuckin' believe it. 'Cause if you don't, you're gonna be sorry. Seriously fuckin' sorry. You hear me? I'm not fuckin' around, I'm serious. You'd better disappear, and soon, or you're gonna regret it. You're gonna fuckin' pay.' This one rattled me. As I say, I get threats all the time. Just not usually this close to home, or hot off the press, to speak.

Dialling 1471 got me nothing: withheld number. As expected. It did tell me that the call had been made just ten minutes ago, though. Of course, it could have just been guesswork, but the timing and the fact that it made accurate reference to my recent movements was something that made me think it wasn't.

So who was this? I'd have to give it some thought. If I hadn't put away several shots already, I'd be reaching for the whiskey right now. I wasn't shaking – I'm too accustomed to this kind of shit by now – but I was feeling a little hot under the lipstick-smeared collar. It wasn't a look I appreciated.

I took notes of all the messages before erasing them. I make it a habit to record as much detail as possible. About everything, all the time. It's imperative to keep tabs on thing in this line of work. Names, places, dates, times. Some might say it requires a special type of obsessive to do this work successfully. I'd agree with that. But just because I record all that information doesn't mean I'm going to divulge it. It's for me to know and no-one else to find out. I use it as necessary. As appropriate. As I consider appropriate. It's not appropriate to share any more than is strictly and absolutely necessary. Or any more than I'm strictly paid for. No, I never give away anything I don't have to, that I'm not paid for. And I never dispose of anything either. You never know when the most obscure snippet that seems to have absolutely no relevance or use at the time may become absolutely essential, central, pivotal. It happens all the time. Usually about 10 years after the fact. Things have a habit of connecting, of being linked. I don't believe in coincidence.

I only give out my office address on a need-to-know basis. Safest that way. Even then, there are risks, but of course, I can't not have an office, and I certainly can't work from home – wherever that may be at any given time. I tend not to remain at the same domestic address for too long. It's safest that way. Besides, it doesn't do to get too settled. I have all correspondence sent to a PO Box address. But sometimes the whereabouts of my office gets leaked into the wrong ears. The number of times I've had the place turned over, I've lost count, although I do of course have the details recorded and on file. Needless to say, they always leave empty handed. As if I'd be stupid enough to leave anything of importance at the office. The place is practically bare. I'm talking a desk, a phone, a basic PC with internet connection, a couple of chairs and very little else. There used to be a kettle, but that ceased to function recently and I've been too busy to replace it. It doesn't bother me too much: the place just a few doors away does more than reasonable takeaway coffee and I'm not big on tea or smoothies or any of that shit.

All of my files are vaulted, with backups vaulted elsewhere in strategically and secretly located safes and gun cabinets. I don't even store information on the hard drive of the PC in the office and use an external one instead that I detach and stow in a separate secure location when not in use. And I have a number of other external hard drives where I back up this information. They too are stored in separate secure locations.

I need distraction. I need to clear my head. I need to work. I fire up the PC and scan the news headlines while waiting for the coffee to cool. I take the bottle of bourbon from the desk drawer and slip a nip into the brew. Ok, probably not the best idea under the circumstances, but hey. At least the room-temperature liquor – I maintain the office at a steady 22°, being fortunate enough to have both heating and air-con – will help cool the intensely hot beverage in the double-lined cardboard cup. I give it a quick swirl with the wooden stick that was sitting on my desk from a previous visit to the coffee house. Ok, so I'm a hoarder, but there are worse traits. You never know when things might come in handy. Moments like this justify these squirreling tendencies.

I swear the world's going mad. Scratch that: it's gone mad. Completely, utterly, irrevocably. We're screwed. But hey, it keeps me in work. The headline 'Man had boss killed to save job' catches my eye so I light a cigarette and read on.

*Spanish police have arrested a man whom they suspect hired a contract killer to murder his boss in a desperate bid to avoid being laid off, newspaper El Pais reported on Tuesday.*

*The head of audiovisual services at the Barcelona International Convention Centre contracted a Colombian man who shot and killed the director of the convention centre on Feb 9, according to police.*

*The director had planned to lay off the arrested man as part of a restructuring project, police said.*

*In fear of losing his job, the head of services, through his sister, contracted a team of six Colombians who planned and carried out the killing, El Pais reported.*

*Police have also detained the sister and six Colombians.*

*The shooting marks one of the most extreme actions by Spaniards who fear losing jobs, homes and businesses during a recession in which unemployment is rising faster than in any other developed country.*

*Other cases include an indebted Spanish builder who kidnapped his bank manager at gunpoint and the head of a construction firm who threatened to set himself on fire unless debts he was owed were paid.*

This kind of crazy shit rarely seemed to go down over here in Britain. I wondered if there was any particular reason for this. Perhaps there really is a prevailing lack of passion and the international reputation for being reserved is justified. Perhaps it was the climate. Everyone seems to go a bit whappy when the mercury rises above 25°C. The chavs whip of their shirts, people start shaking their inhibitions, start getting a bit aggro.

# 11

I continue to work my way through the files stored on Jackson Jr's memory sticks, and through the cigarettes I bought earlier. Oh ho ho, he's got some on-line Internet accounts – Yahoo and Google – and his usernames and passwords are stored on a single Word document. What a bozo, no concept of security. I'll probably find his Internet banking details before long. I sign into his Google account. Precious little: looks like he'd been using it as a dumping ground for junk mails, all the things he'd signed up to buy didn't want to have to flitter all the crap for. Competition entries, all the rest. And porn. So much porn. I was naturally curious so checked out some of the links. Not my scene, but it's true what they say about getting inside the mind of a criminal or whatever. To hunt, you have to get closer to the hunted. Whatever it takes.

Jackson was evidently a kinky old bastard. The hardcore stuff was one thing, but pretty standard in real terms. Cumshots, anal, pretty tedious really. There was a fair bit of light BDSM material, too.

'Oh bondage, up yours,' I sneered as I rifled through some of the pathetic teenage fantasies being played out before a photographer.

But the reams of somnophiliac material was rather disturbing. Sure, much of it was quite clearly staged, but even so.... who the fuck gets off on fucking someone in their sleep? I couldn't see how this was any different from rape. It's a sick, sick world. I often felt that I wanted no part of it. Trouble was, my line of work drags me back and puts me in contact with some of the nastiest, seediest, most fucked-up half-lives around. You couldn't make them up. The shit I've seen... I should be entirely desensitised by now. Or deranged. Maybe I'm both and don't realise it. But then every once in a while something comes along that really slaps you round the chops. It leaves you numb. The sickness never ends. It's a plague.

What struck me was the technical detail surrounding these unsavoury practices, with many of the sites doing into extraordinary detail about the background and medical terminologies. The text outweighed the images on many pages. Knowledge is power, so I read. And I read. After all, I had only a cursory knowledge of these perversions, mostly gleaned from Roger.


1. Somnophilia (Sleepysex): arousal by fondling or having sex with someone who is sleeping.

2. Somnophilia: fondling a stranger in their sleep.

3. Somnophilia: the sleeping princess syndrome, a paraphilia of the marauding/predatory type in which erotic arousal and facilitation or attainment of orgasm are responsive to and contingent on intruding on and awakening a sleeping partner or stranger with erotic caresses, including oral sex, not involving force or violence [from Latin, somnus, sleep + philia, love or obsession).

Note: There is no technical term for the reciprocal paraphilic condition of being the recipient, which occurs more readily in fantasy than in actuality.

1. Sleeping Princess Syndrome (SPS): those aroused by partner who is sleeping or appears to be asleep.

1. Paraphilia: abnormal sexual activity.

2. Paraphilia: a condition in which a person's sexual arousal and gratification depend on fantasizing about and engaging in sexual behavior that is atypical and extreme.

3. Paraphilia: medical or behavioral science term for what is also referred to as: sexual deviation, sexual anomaly, sexual perversion or a disorder of sexual preference.

Note: Research has shown paraphilic behaviors occur with high frequency. They are found almost exclusively in males and tend to have their onset during puberty. Paraphilias are reported in many cultures and have long been reported or described throughout history.

1. Sexual Perversion: an aberrant sexual practice that is preferred to "normal" sexual desire or intercourse.

Below all of this, there was no shortage of images. Thumbnail upon thumbnail, linking to galleries, and links to various somnophiliac blogs and even an array of sleepsploitation videos of men sticking their circumcised penesis and a host of other objects – often vegetables – into the vaginas and anuses of supposedly sleeping women.

This was pretty tame compared to what I found next. So, Jackson didn't just like his pleasures dark, he liked them darker still. I sat agog as I read the header blurb on this next site:

Tit torture, nipple torture and breast bondage is what you're here for. We've got thousands of exclusive pictures of bound and tortured breasts, hundreds of original stories of punished tits and nipples, art and drawings, video and movie clips, prints and more. From sensual and erotic to severe, cruel, extreme, and brutal, Darker Pleasures has done nothing but breast bondage and tit and nipple torture since 1999.

I wince. There's a helluva lot of text and mercifully few pictures, at least on this homepage, although the menus at the top and right of the page offer movies, galleries and stories. I light a cigarette. I wince again, but read on.

## 12

The Malleus Maleficarum, a manual purported by some to have been read more widely than the bible, and arguably seen as the authority during the entire 250 years of the Inquisition, went into great detail on the process by which witches were located, interrogated, and tortured. When discussing the breasts and nipples, the two holy priests that wrote it noted that they were "extremely sensitive, on account of the refinement of the veins."

In actuality, it is widely accepted that both the secular and pious souls that did the torturing probably enjoyed every moment. And when their enjoyment became too obvious, and the pup tent was pitched, they simply said that the hapless "witch" had cast a spell on them, and proceeded to lay waste to the tormented bosom that much more.

I'm not using the term "lay waste" metaphorically. Many of the toys and torments I'm about to talk about have been documented over and over again in the annals of time. Others rely a bit more on speculation, but I haven't found anyone yet that would argue against the probability that I'm right. It doesn't take a rocket scientist, after all.

Among the first toys we find used by our medieval tit torturers were such things as the cat claw.

This metal claw was used to rake flesh, in most cases turning a pair of tits into something basically resembling shredded wheat. While we'd never condone this practice, the Inquistitors had pretty much been given carte blanche, and they had an unlimited supply of witches from whom to choose. After all, they had only to pick a lovely pair of breasts and grease some lying palm before the accusations would fly and their divine work was at hand.

Now, while the cat claw could be used on body parts besides the breasts, the breast ripper had just one use - hence the name. Since there were a variety of sizes of breasts from which to choose, so came a variety of sizes of rippers. But regardless of size, their intended use couldn't be mistaken. Placed against the base of the breast and twisted and... well, it doesn't take a genius to figure that one out. As an added bonus, they frequently stored them in hot coals until their use so as to heat the metal red or white hot. No, it wasn't to keep them sterile to avoid infection.

The cousin of the breast ripper was called the spider. This ingenious little gadget worked the same way, but it could be adjusted so that smaller targets could be coerced. Instead of latching into the whole breasts, devout men could concentrate on just the tips, playing rough with a fine nipple and areola until the evil witch confessed, typically just after she was divested of said nipple.

It was found that the torturer frequently bit or otherwise chewed on the witche's nipple before applying any of these friendly devices, ostensibly to make them more tender and ripe for a quicker confession once the spider was applied.

Not every holy torturer preferred such

blatant rending. For the more subtle ones, there were a wide variety of crushing devices. Among them was a very large and heavy wooden spiked device that had originally been made to puree hands and feet. There's little doubt that other uses were found that catered to those with fetishes of the non-foot kind.

Thumbscrews crushed nipples, too.

Just like the shredding and ripping devices, clamping tools came in a variety of sizes in order to cater to the needs of the holy torturer. If a priest, in his infinite wisdom, believed that it would be best to extract a confession by way of only the nipple and its surrounds, instead of through the whole tamale, then the thumbscrew worked quite well. Designed to play havoc with the digits, nipples and areola frequently found themselves the subject of Inquisitional puree, as it were.

By now you might see why so many women confessed to being witches. If this had been modern times, we'd have been able to find the Lindbergh baby's kidnapper, learn the truth behind the Kennedy assassination, and get the real scoop about Area 51 with just the removal of a bra.

Those of us familiar with modern day, politically correct tit torture, have probably found some similarities between the toys used in the enlightened times of the Crusades and today's more barbaric BDSM play. And with those similarities, I'd be remiss if I didn't mention many a dom's favorite pastime - flogging. Now, while we usually stick with the pansy-ass stuff, those educated priests really knew how to flog, and metal was the flagellating material of choice.

They called these chain-made floggers, "scourges." Most of them were simply wooden handles with several lengths of chain attached. The more ingenious of the bunch might attach spiked balls to the ends, or for the really up and coming, the entire chain would be spiked, rather like barbed wire.

I think the operative phrase for any unfortunate breast owner that found herself the object of attention for one of these would be, "Witch? Me? Oh, yeah!"

Like everything else we've talked about with modern equivalents, other fun torments we use today found their roots way back when. Piercing, for example, was also a prevalent method of witch torture. Since sterile needles weren't in fashion, anything sharp and pointy usually served. And while the truly adventurous among us might dabble in the occasional fish hook through the nubbin, these guys much preferred the meat hooking variety. Not to be barbaric, all of these, like the rippers, were often subject to hot coals. And if the implements weren't, then the pert objects of their attention may well have been.

Another fun toy used to keep "witches" at arm's length -- at least in public -- in the belief that it was dangerous for the morally upright to touch a "witch," was the "Witch Catcher." Several different devices have borne the same name, but in this case it was essentially a type of modified pole-arm. The point was used to push the accused, while the hook was used to bring the accused back to control. The protective phrase "Jesus Nazarenum and Ave Maria" was frequently inscribed upon the hook for further protection.

The witch catcher wasn't the only pole arm that could be used to toy with tits. Soldiers with spears regularly toyed with the targets that tended to attract the most attention, and while it's a little known fact that most women were crucified facing the cross, breasts could be had from any direction.

One of the most notorious devices of any era was the guillotine, invented in the 1700s. What most people don't know, is that the guillotine had ancestors made many centuries earlier. The Halifax Gibbet was nothing more than an axe head imbedded in a really heavy wooden block that was fixed in grooved uprights and dropped on the hapless victim. While history recalls most of these victims being severed at the neck, a variety of these have been made that work on other body parts, breasts being a big hit at the many witch hunt carnivals of the times.

But such devices were unwieldy, and lacked the personal touch many distinguished torturers of the time preferred. Because of this, other means were devised for more selective nipple and breast removal. Don't say you're surprised.

Well before the pliers and vice grips that modern day practitioners employ, there were a couple of devices that tended toward a more permanent ending to nipple play. Those were called the tongue tearers and mutilation shears. Given the names, I could probably leave what they did to your imagination and move on, but that would make this a very short article, wouldn't it? Although called "tongue tearers," these sharpened plier-like devices were as likely to be used on the tips of breasts and given pet names like "Betty." Mutilation shears were more like handle-less scissors, and tended to sever things a little more quickly.

Both of these playful tools came with screws so they could be slowly and deliberately closed, drawing out the fun so the lucky lady had plenty of time to consider how she might best phrase her confession for the audience.

Other types of tongs and pinchers frequently found their way into the arsenals of tools used to convince confessions from the mouths of witches. Fireplace tongs, horseshoing pliers, and all manner of squishing things were used on nipples and various other parts of the female anatomy in order to reach the desired goal.

Like other tools, tongs were specifically adapted as well. Inquisitioners would pay to have spurs and teeth cut into specially-made tongs for easier, and far more painful, nipple ripping. Masters of torture could spend hours nipping away at a woman's breasts, first bruising and ultimately tearing them away piece by piece. As luck would have it, we just happen to have full-color slide shows of exactly this sort of thing taking place. We just can't show them here.

Anyway, keeping the world safe from paganism and extracting penance from women who didn't know their own mind was a time consuming and sometimes dirt job, of course. With laundry maids likely becoming a rare commodity, given the large numbers of them that were witches, it's speculated that private sessions became clothing-optional affairs, saving the clergy and the church the cost of cleaning blood and other body fluids from the holy garments.

Having read the history I began to wonder if the sickos who surfed sites like this got off as much on the intellectualization of their perversions, or if they somehow managed to kid themselves that it wasn't fucked up simply because these antics had the weight of history behind them to 'justify' them somehow. Yeah, yeah, it's a fine line between art and pornography and all that, but this shit was truly beyond the pale.

Some of it was subscription stuff, and very, very hard. I don't shock easily, but some of what I'd seen was way, way much. But there was something that troubled me about these sites, just as something troubled me about the last message on my answerphone. No time to think about it now, though. It had gone 19:00 and I had a couple of hours' drive to get to the Jackson's summerhouse. Scratching my itch could wait.

## 13

I pulled up at the driveway to the Jackson's lakeside summerhouse at 21:16. The sky was beginning to cloud, and  darkness was finally descending as the developing layer of altostratus. It wasn't the best sign. These middle level clouds are composed of ice crystals and water droplets and often form ahead of storms that will produce continuous precipitation.

Sunset had been at 20:22, after 14h 34m 59s of daylight hours. The days were drawing in by a couple or so minutes at either end of the day, but the sky stayed light and the air was humid: 85% humidity had been the average over the last week. The moon was rising and would attain an altitude of 52.3° from London at solar noon. It was 151.492 ($10^6$ km) from the earth at this point in its cycle, as it entered its first quarter. I wanted to have a quick reccy before going in for the kill.  Metaphorically, that is. How little did I know... anyway. For this operation I needed the cover of darkness. Can never be too careful. Perhaps I should've worn black. Perhaps I should've brought my Mac.

Having scouted round the grounds, I decide to move the car to a spot a little further up the road. Ok, so perhaps I'm paranoid. So sue me. I've seen enough to know that my paranoia's always justified. I prefer to call it self-preservation. That's why I'm packing on this mission, too.

The car hidden off road behind a patch of gorse bushes, I proceed on to the summerhouse. I don't go straight up the drive, though. Too exposed.

I steal along the edge of the well-tended grounds on the long approach to the building that stands at the lakeside.

Arriving at the building, I'm still half-surprised by its size. It's not only bigger than my two-up two-down, but probably has a comparable floorspace to my pad plus the next three either side. I'm guessing in the region of 2,000sq. ft. for the ground floor. Immense. No wonder Mrs. Jackson's not too bothered about the tab. I cross the decking and peer in through the French windows. Much of the ground floor is open plan, with polished wooden floors – none of that ersatz laminate shit – with expensive-looking rugs placed strategically before the leather sofas and glass-topped coffee tables.

I move round, cautiously. The partition walls separate the living area from the open plan kitchen / diner. It's from this vantage as I look in though the window, trying to decide the best port of entry that I spot movement within. A thin shaft of torchlight. Having started at the right side of the house, I've worked my way across the front and can see to the left side, where there is, I learned during my preliminary casing of the joint, a second track wide enough to facilitate vehicular access. I'd considered coming down that way myself, but was concerned that I could find myself trapped if another vehicle followed after me. I was sure I could hear something off in that direction. I tried filtering out the different sounds. The lap of the water on the beach to the front of the house – which was why there was only front and side access, plus a small footpath down to the boathouse and jetty – was the main sound. The breeze in the trees that lined the shore. The occasional hoot of an owl. It was pretty quiet this far from anywhere. But I could sense something and the hairs on the back of my neck stood on end.

The torch beam again. Someone was at the foot of the stairs and making their way to the side door. That someone was dressed in black, like a sniper or SAS trooper. I ducked back behind the corner of the building as he stole his way out of the door, keeping an eye on his movements from my obscured vantage.

Then, without warning, the crack of a pistol being fired shattered the tranquil night air. The sound ricocheted off the house before being subdued by the inky water. The burglar dropped to the ground. A figure sprang from the bushes and made straight for the prostrate body. This figure was also dressed entirely in black. It was hard to make much out in the dark, other than that, judging by its height and bulk, it was male.

He frisked the burglar, who put up no resistance. At that moment, the air was rent once more by the sound of an engine firing up and the scene was illuminated as a pair of double headlamps came on, flooding the darkness with a blinding halogen glare. A vehicle – a 4x4 – was parked in the narrow lane that ran to the house, parallel to the coastline of the lake. The gunman prized something from the slain burglar's hand. Then he stood up and bot the boot in, hard – once, twice, three times – to the fallen man's genitals, stomach and finally face, before leaping up and sprinting to the waiting vehicle. The powerful engine roared as the driver threw it into reverse, then pulled a sharp 1-point turn a few metres further from the house where the track widened momentarily – a passing place. Within seconds, the taillights had retreated out of range and the near silence was once again restored.

I'm momentarily frozen. What had I just seen here? Some guy jumps out of the bushes, shoots a guy who's just leaving a place he's broken into and left with next to nothing, then bails into a vehicle and races off... and what am I supposed to do? Complete my mission, of course. The coast looks pretty clear now, at least. Apart from the guy lying in the doorway, that is. I move to where he's lying an immediately recognise him as Tommy Cook. I check his neck for a pulse. He's as dead as a doornail.

There's a rapidly expanding puddle of thin, watery-looking blood that shines black in the moonlight, pooling at the back of his head. Small wonder this anaemic-looking tosser's blood looks thin: approximately 90% of plasma is water, with the rest composed of dissolved substances, primarily proteins (e.g. albumin, globulin, fibronogen). Plasma typically accounts for 55% by volume of blood and of the remaining 45% the greatest contribution is from the red blood cells. This malnourished Pot Noodle-eating weasel was likely no more than 35% red blood cells. 55% plasma, 10% jissom.

The shooter was either a good shot or fluky as fuck: there's an entry wound in Cook's throat.

His face is badly broken where the killer's boot connected. Must've been steel-toed to do this much damage with a single jab: he's taken out a couple of teeth and cracked his nose, from which twin rivulets of blood are flowing from the nostrils and down the side of his face.

'That's what you get for messin' with the big boys,' I tell him. He doesn't hear. He's dead.

I slip into the summerhouse through the open door. The little cock-end's saved me the trouble of breaking in, and I'm grateful for that. Ok, grateful's perhaps a bit strong. Thankful? Relieved? Yeah, more like it. I flick on my flashlight and scan the downstairs rooms, which scream minimalist opulence. Even in the gloom it's clear that the finishing and detail is something else. I quickly surmise that anything that may be of use won't be down here though, and make my way up the stairs, two at a time. Four palatial bedrooms, all en-suite lead off from the landing. The first three look pretty standard, but the fourth is littered with photographic equipment – backdrops, reflectors, that sort of thing – but no cameras. Looks like it's been used as a studio for a photoshoot. A strange sense of déjà vu shivers fleetingly through my cerebral cortex. Something I just can't place... I shrug it off. I've work to do.

There's another room off the back of this one. It's pretty sparsely furnished, containing a desk, a couple of chairs and a large filing cabinet. The place had been turned over. Already.

'Shit,' I cursed the air.

Beaten by Cook the Crook, who had in turn

been beaten by someone else, someone as yet unidentified. I had a rifle through the cabinets which were practically empty, and the desk drawers. Nothing to see here... only, I'd have thought Jackson Sr. would have wanted to forget work when he came out here, so an office off one of the bedrooms struck me as odd. Perhaps I just find it hard to believe that someone could be that obsessive about their work. Even more obsessive than myself. None of this explained the photography gear either. Still, there wasn't any sign of anything untoward, and if there had been anything, it had left the building and gone to who knows where in that black SUV.

I was too late, then. Disappointed and angry, I made my way back down the stairs and to the door. I stepped over Cook's corpse and glanced down at him as I did so. Exanguination had drained his skin to the colour of alabaster. I felt nothing as I walked slowly to my car back up by the road. It was going to be a long drive home. I put the pedal to the metal. The roads were clear and the speedo soon rose to a readily sustainable 75mph.

## 14

I didn't go home. I needed to go home and I needed to sleep. I needed a shower and I needed a clean shirt. Which meant I needed to do some laundry. But my mind wasn't going to let me rest, and nor was the case. Things were starting to hot up. Not that I could piece anything together from what I had: two dead guys, one a big money guy, the other a no-mark bullshit artist, two missing guys, a hot client, a ton of dangerous-looking porn, a Subaru with blacked-out windows and a threat that sounded like it was serious amongst the usual crap on my answerphone.

I lit a cigarette as I pondered. What had Cook lifted from the summerhouse when he'd turned it over? What was it that was so valuable that they'd kill to get it? What the hell had Jackson been up to before he disappeared? So many questions and so few answers. All of these questions brought me back to the reason I was involved in all of this in the first place. Where was Jackson, and why had he gone missing?

I fired up the PC and poured myself three fingers of J.D. from the bottle I keep in my desk drawer. No, I'm not an alcoholic, although you could hardly blame me if I was. The things I've seen would be enough to turn any man to booze. I'll admit I was rattled after tonight's events. I couldn't help thinking that the bullet was intended for me. Or at least, that I'd've been the recipient if I'd arrived at the summerhouse first. After all, the guy who took whatever it was from the dead guy didn't stop to chat or to see if the burglar had whatever it was he wanted. No, he shot first and didn't even ask any questions later. The hit had been executed with clinical, brutal precision.

Something was bugging me about Jackson Jr.'s porn stash. Ok, so a lot of things were bugging me about Jackson Jr.'s porn stash, and a lot of things were bugging me about a lot of things. The further I got into this case, the harder it became to see where I was going. I wondered if I wasn't getting distracted by all the Jackson Jr. shit, but I had a hunch that there was no tackling one without the other. Besides, I'd been there when he'd croaked. How could I not have an interest? The two were clearly related, and I don't just mean paternally. Call it detective instinct. I don't expect a clear view at all times, but this one was getting foggier the more it unravelled.

It was anything but foggy outside, though. The cloud cover that had come down over the lake hadn't built up here. The blinds that cover the window in my office were adjusted so I could see out. There was no traffic and the streetlights seemed crisper and starker than usual as they illuminated the clear August sky of perfect midnight blue. I sunk the J.D. as the PC warmed up and poured myself another couple of fingers.

I stuck Jackson's memory stick into one of the USB ports at the front of the unit. Using the usernames and passwords supplied, I scanned some of the pictures on the sites again. No, not for kicks. Something about those websites had been playing on my mind on the journey back.

Bingo! For starters, the layouts of many of the sites was similar, even identical. That in itself wasn't all that surprising. Many of these porn sites are run by the same people. By spreading the material, so to speak, they were increasing market potential. It pays to cater to all tastes, it's good business sense. So there were porn empires on line, with some operations running literally hundreds of sites, all linking to one another.

I scanned the files on the memory stick again and found a file within a file containing a .zip file that contained a whole host of details I'd missed. More account details. Same sites, but not user access this time. No, these were webmaster passes. So Jackson Jr. was either solely or jointly behind a porn empire catering to the sadistic and the perverted? Stranger things have happened, but even so, this one surprised me.

I brought up an Internet browser and went to domaincrawler.com. Sites like this are invaluable when it comes to doing detective work these days. And people simply don't realise just how much information they're making available in the public domain. Within seconds, I had the IP addresses for the bulk of the sites, as well as the name, address and telephone numbers of the people they were registered to, as well as site-associated email addresses and secondary access details.

That strange sense of déjà vu had been eating at me too. There was something familiar about that room in the summerhouse. And there it was, right there, on screen, before my very eyes.

Some of the shoots had been done in that very room! Granted, they were mostly the tamer ones – the light bondage and so on, rather than the extreme torture sets that had been shot in various locations that looked like dungeons (presumably they were only sets, but some did look pretty convincing). Even so...

## 15

I spend the rest of the night through to the small hours combing the subfolders of Jackson Jr.'s memory sticks. The ashtray was spilling out over the desk long before dawn. However, I'd managed to crack the codes that enabled me to access his computer remotely, and, from there, Jackson Sr.'s. Maybe I'd actually start making some kind of progress at last. I was concerned I'd squandered a disproportionate amount of time on Jackson Jr. and a host of dead ends and wanted to have something to report back to Jacinta when we next spoke. She'd told me she was heading out of town in the morning, which meant in the next few hours, and she'd be gone for a couple of days. This bought me some time, but I just wanted to feel like I was getting somewhere. Shit was going down and I had to be quick or be dead. And if not me, then some other sucker. There was a trail of devastation forming in my wake. It was a worry.

Trawling through endless business reports and spreadsheets was a real chew, and most of his emails were as dull as they were above board. So, was Jackson Sr. keeping business and pleasure separate after all? Not that it mattered entirely. I'd got enough on his seedy underground activities to know he wasn't the man he purported to be.

One email in his sent box piqued my interest though. It had been sent to a Natalie Bailey. I was sure I'd seen that name before, too.

*Ever wish you'd done something different? Ever wish you'd done some things differently? Obviously it's too late for regret, as it won't change anything and is simply a needless expenditure of energy and there's less to spare as each year passes but do you? Do you have regrets? A yearning to go back and change things? Or would you play out the mistakes the same anyway: after all, we learn from our mistakes and know not to make them again. Even so, there's always that small wish to go back, retrace the steps taken in blindness and rectify some of those darker moments those moments, however fleeting, of the most acute embarrassment... isn't there? Or is it just me?*

*I don't wish to change who I am, or what I've 'become' – I probably couldn't anyway, there seems to be an inevitability about the path we tread, and fight circumstance as hard as me might, it feels like a losing battle. People do us over, finance and situations of employment, family, all unwittingly contrive to bring us to the present whatever we do. But don't you sometimes think 'what if?'*

*What if you'd gone what that guy or that girl what if you'd been less spineless in relenting to that push or that, what if you'd not given in so easily when told 'no' to that, what if you had applied for this job, that job and the other job? If you'd not given up after the fifteenth knock-back on one career or another, had held on to and fought harder to cling to one dream or another?*

*Or when you discover that you're finally able to make progress of sorts? Don't you wish that you'd been the person you are now a decade ago? Or even fifteen years ago? What would you change? What would you have done differently? What were your dreams? Do you still have any of them now?*

*And how about the way you look? What would you change? Anything? Nothing? How do you feel about the ageing process? How do you feel now about your childhood? How much of it can you actually remember?*

*I find that I feel that while my memory is still as good as ever, some recollections are becoming somehow distorted. Or perhaps it's that I struggle to reconcile them with my adult self.*

*I don't miss the lack of responsibility of childhood. I was as repressed as a teenager as I am now. I wish I had evolved differently. I wish I'd been the person I am now or feel I'm becoming then, ten, fifteen years ago. Don't you ever wish that? How would you be with the people you knew then if you were how you are now? Were there missed opportunities? Did you not speak when you should have done? Did you say things when you'd have been better not doing? Or simply say the wrong thing? How would you replay it?*

*I'd replay it all in slow motion and consider my moves for a start. And do it from my perspective now. But there's no going back… is there?*

'Repressed?' There was no reply in Jackson's inbox. Perhaps it was nothing. What aroused my interest was the sheer strangeness of the message. It wouldn't be entirely unreasonable to surmise from this that Jackson, who was knocking on, it had to be said – at least in relation to his wife - was having an affair and something of a breakdown to boot. You saw it all the time. These rich bastards who get to the long end of middle age and don't like it. These rich bastards who can buy their way out of it, at least for a while. Money can't buy you happiness, but it can buy you delusion.

It's been getting steadily lighter for a good few hours now and I check my watch. It's stopped. I check the clock on the PC. The coffee shop down the road will be open in another five minutes. I'm wrecked through lack of sleep and need a strong brew, so gather up my coat and head down the street at a sedate pace. I need the air. I need a breather. I need to give my eyes a break from the screen. I've been staring at it for about five hours straight now.

No sooner have I returned with my hot strong black Americano – five sugars – than there's a knock at the door.

'What the fuck?' I mutter to myself under my breath. Very few people know where the office is located.

I'm hanging my coat up when there's another rap, harder and louder this time.

'Alright, alright,' I grumble.

'Hello? Police! Anyone there?'

I open the door. 'What the hell's going on?' I grizzle. I don't like being disturbed, especially when I've not had my caffeine fix.

'Mr. Thunder.' It's DCI Bradley, and he's brought a couple of uniforms with him. Subtle.

'What is it?' Fucking coppers. I don't even know why he feels the need to turn up like this. I'd left him my details and my card and told him to call me if there was anything else he needed to ask, although I'd made it clear I'd given him all I'd got and that I was as in the dark about the mysterious sudden death of Jackson Jr. as the next man. Bradley had given me his card and insisted I ring him if I remembered anything, or the moment I learned anything that might help him in his investigations. Wasn't the fact I hadn't called enough to suggest I hadn't got anything for him? Clearly not.

Bradley was OK most of the time, but when the pressure was on or when he had a case that looked like becoming high-profile, he had a knack of turning into a supreme cunt and chucking his weight around.

'Mr. Thunder, I'd like you to accompany me to the station, please. I have a few questions I'd like to ask you in connection with the death of Joseph Jackson,' he puffs officiously.

'Can't you ask me here?' I growl.

'I'm afraid not,' he panders.

'What? Are you arresting me?' I explode. I don't have time for this shit. I'm tired, I'm hungry and I've got work to do. And I want my fucking coffee.

'No, no,' Bradley breezed, 'we just want to have this all on record, properly. Procedure, you understand.'

'I understand alright,' I grumped. 'I'll get my coat.'

'Thank you,' Bradley said pompously with a hit of smugness. He wasn't doing much of a job of hiding the fact he got off on this kind of power trip. He'd obviously watched too many episodes of 'The Bill' and all that TV cop show shit. I wanted to punch him in the chops, but thought better of it. I wanted to get in and out as quickly as possible and didn't need the extra hassle of being charged with assaulting a police officer. Even if he was a power-tripping moron.

'Can I bring my coffee?' I ask with more than just a hint of sarcasm.

'Sure,' he acquiesced, completely missing it.

I was glad it was early. It meant no-one was about to see me bundled into a car and taken down the cop shop.

They kept me waiting an interminably long time. Because I was there 'voluntarily' I was left to loiter in reception and ignored by the desk staff who made like they were busy but were, as far as I could determine, busy idling and not a lot else.

It's 11:58:43 when a uniform summons me and leads me to one of the interview rooms. I've consumed several litres of coffee from the machine while I've been waiting, and while the stuff is piss-weak instant shit dispensed in 250ml cups that are only 80% full, I've sunk nine of the things – I'm useless when it comes to killing time – and consequently, with 1.8l of coffee in me, I'm totally wired.

'Mr. Thunder,' Bradley booms in his most authoritative tone as he paced the room with his hands on his belt.

'Inspector Bradley,' I echo, unfazed.

'As you're aware, you were the last person to see Joseph Jackson alive. That much we've established.'

I nod. It doesn't seem to warrant a reply.

'So...' another plain-clothes I don't know

and haven't been properly introduced to wanders over from the far corner. 'We want you to run us through your meeting with him again. Making sure you don't miss anything out.'

'I already did that,' I sigh.

'Indulge us,' Anonymous Plain-Clothes says, leaning on the table, his face closer to mine than I'm comfortable with.  His breath is rank, like a compost-heap, stale fags and cheap coffee. But then, I guess mine's not much better right now. I've not had a lot of time for things like teeth-cleaning in the past 24 hours.

'Must I?' I groan.

'If you wouldn't mind,' whines Bradley impatiently.

I do, but I run through events again, practically verbatim. I'm well practised at this sort of thing. I'm about halfway through, and have just reached the point at which Jackson's starting to wobble for the first time when Anonymous Plain-Clothes interjects.

'The autopsy's revealed that Mr. Jackson was poisoned,' he says baldly.

'Ok,' I say flatly, unfazed. I might've guessed that. I was there, after all, and I've seen heart attacks and strokes. I knew it was neither.

'What time did you say you arrived?' Bradley presses.

'I had an appointment for 10:30. I arrived early: 10:20.' I wasn't about to give him the extra minute and a half. 'Jackson kept me waiting till five minutes or so after the allotted time.'

'And how long had you been in his

presence before you say he began to manifest the symptoms you described earlier?' Bradley pomped.

'Not long. A matter of minutes. Seven to ten. I wasn't in there long. He was dead within, what fifteen, twenty minutes.'

'Can you be more precise?' Bradley's putting on the thumbscrews, leaning over me across the table while his colleague makes a show of circling like a vulture ready to swoop for the prey.

I chew it over briefly. I could be more precise. But I can't. Shan't. Won't. That would expose the lag between Jackson snuffing it and me making the call. That would lay me open to further suspicion, and I'm not about to give these law enforcers any more ammo. I'm not about to admit to having gone over the office before making the call either.

'I'm afraid not,' I say, shaking my head apologetically. I'm keeping tight-lipped on this one, no matter what.

Bradley tries a different tack. 'Did you see anyone leave before you entered Mr. Jackson's office?'

'No.'

'Are you sure?' Anonymous Plain-Clothes.

'Positive.' I shifted uncomfortably in my chair. It wasn't that I was feeling the pressure: it was insufferably hot and I needed to pass water. Or coffee, to be precise.

'Are you *sure?*' Anonymous Plain-Clothes bangs his fist on the table. He's flushed, the capillaries around his eyes and in his cheeks are fit to burst with corpuscles racing to the surface. His left eyelid flickers, indicating a collapsed synapse.

I stay calm. 'Yes. Absolutely. But just because I didn't see anyone doesn't mean there wasn't anyone. I took the stairs to Jackson's office. There are two set of stairs that I know of in that building, plus three lifts. Then you've got the fire escapes and trade lifts. C'mon, you figure it out.' I was getting pretty riled up. Did I have to do all the thinking for these imbeciles?

The interview continued for another hour and three quarters. Having gone over the same ground no less than fifteen times, I'd had a gutful.

'Look, are we done here?' I challenged, aggressed. I was itching to get the hell out of there, and not just because of the heat – an insufferable 29°C – or the caffeine which had sent my BP soaring from its standard 'borderline' status of 140/90 to 160/100 which sat on the cusp between mild stage one and moderate stage two hypertension. Bradley was getting under my skin. More importantly, I had work to do: I needed to get out of there and get on with things – before anyone else wound up dead.

Bradley looked at Anonymous Plain-Clothes and they nodded mutually. 'We're done,' Bradley confirmed.

I exhaled a sigh of relief and made my way out of the station. It was a bit of a hike back to the office, but I was fed up of being cooped up, so elected to walk it anyway. I'd be back at the office in roughly 20 minutes anyway. It was a pleasant if hot afternoon: 27°C, 3mph south-westerly breeze, humidity 90%, a high, almost of the scale, pollen count. Sticky. But it was all good with me. I'd managed to stay schtum and it had paid off: Bradley had inadvertently let slip the toxic concoction that had slain Jackson Jr. while it wasn't much to go on, I was confident I could unravel something of use from a snippet like that.

## 16

The poison thing was niggling me when I arrived back at the office. I was a little out of breath from the walk. Not because I'm out of shape, but because the combination of high humidity – sitting at a stagnant treacle-like 90% – and alveoli-clogging pollution hanging heavy in the air made it harder to draw and absorb oxygen. I daresay the three cigarettes I'd smoked on the way hadn't helped much. I was sweating profusely: it was no cooler outside than in that sauna of an interview room they'd spent three hours and 12 minutes grilling me. I also needed to piss. The coffee had gone through my system and had filled by bladder to its full 800ml capacity. Fully distended and with the fluids contained therein creating an almost unbearable pressure, I had crossed the 150ml – 300ml point of micturation quite some time ago.

Of course, you hear about people being poisoned all the time. Like that kid whose parents supposedly poisoned him with salt, and Alexander Litvinenko's assassination by radiation poisoning, which unravelled like a classic thriller. But most of the time it is the stuff of fiction. And while the details of Jackson's toxicology report that that bozo Bradley had let slip had given me something to chew on, even the police wouldn't have had all that much to go on. It's not fucking *CSI*. You don't get to know the exact composition of everything, and what rare ingredient that only a couple of people in the whole city had access to was featured in the profile. It's impossible to determine the precise minute it was ingested, too, so none of that being caught on CCTV leaving one venue and arriving at another and then again being caught in the lift on the way out having administered that last fix.

So there was a cocktail of sodium hypochlorite, phenols, chlorinated phenols, carbaryl, dichlorophene, chlordane and other non-specific chlorinated hydrocarbons, methanol and ethylene glycol in Jackson Jr.'s system when he snuffed it. Small wonder he wasn't looking good when I saw him. Any one of those could have been fatal given the right – or wrong – dosage.

I stopped short at the door. I was sure I'd closed it and locked up, but there it was, open. Only a crack, but it was still open. I was unarmed and beginning to regret it. Something told me that danger was present. I could smell it lurking in the vicinity.

I leaned back and eased the door open with just the tip of my boot. It swung slowly, silently on its hinges. Silence. Perhaps I'd been mistaken after all. Perhaps in my haste, in being hustled out, I'd forgotten to close the door properly and to lock up. Unlikely.

Cautiously, I crossed the threshold, scanning left, right – as far right as the door, still only half-open would allow – and straight ahead. The place had been turned over. In broad daylight, too! Not that there was much to turn. This is precisely why I keep everything of potential interest stored off premises. Still silence. Looks like I've missed the intruder.

115

Nevertheless, I proceed with caution and enter fully. The desk drawers have been jimmied open and their contents – a few invoices for telephone, electricity and the like for the office, a couple of spare notebooks, business cards (mostly my own plus a few for taxi firms and so on) are scattered about on the tiled floor. The PC's on and has been left open at the 'My documents' panel. As if I'd be so dumb as to leave anything anyone might want in there. Either the intruder got spooked or otherwise got bored having realised there was nothing to be got from this place.

Just then, I heard something. A slight creak. The toilet door? I spun round and caught the side of a man's face peering out to see if the coast was clear. Clearly he'd not been banking on me standing between him and the exit.

In three long, fast strides, I was at the back of the office and at the lavatory door. He instinctively slammed it shut. What was he going to do, stay locked in my toilet till I got bored and went away? I met the door with my shoulder and powered it open with the force of my full body weight, 188.5lbs.

The door swung back and made full contact with his chest and chin, throwing him backwards where he collided with the wall directly behind him. The room was a mere 3 feet across. He simultaneously caught the right ilium of his pelvis against the washbasin with a dull thud. An expression of pain flickered across his face and I was on him instantly, landing a sharp blow to the stomach. The air rushed from his lungs like a paper bag being burst and he doubled over just as I raised my knee. It connected with his face and there was a resounding crack as his left nasal bone shattered into the pulpy matter of his lower lateral cartilages and septum. He howled with pain and snapped his head back up, blood spurting from his nostrils and spraying the off-white walls and crisp white tiles on the floor.

He lunged forward blindly and I tried to side-step his wild flailing blows but there isn't room in this confined space and he caught the side of my head with the knuckles his large right hand, balled into a fist the size of a ham.

Trying to take advantage of this brief respite from my initial onslaught, he makes to barge past me, out into the office. He's halfway through the door when I stick my foot out – a simple but effective move that lands him flat on his face, half in and half out of the minuscule WC.

He groans and has turned himself half over by the time I'm on him, his collars bunched up in my fists.

'Who the fuck are you?' I demand, flecks of spittle spraying from my mouth and onto his face. I can be an animal when I'm angry or threatened. Right now, I'm both. I drive a punch into his mouth. The look on his face tells me that his pain receptors are overloading in response to the blow I've just landed him. I plant another in this throat and can almost see his trachea inflaming instantaneously.

'Fuck you,' he snarls breathlessly through gritted teeth that are red with blood from his nose. He jerks his neck in a wild attempt to headbutt me, but I manage to roll my torso off to one side while keeping his legs pinned with my own.

'Look, you little fucker,' I growl, 'you're gonna talk. Who sent you?' He's a nasty-looking bastard and anything but little: thick-set, burly, at least 250lbs of pumped-up bulk, and well over 6' tall. He's fucking ugly to boot: his beady eyes are close together and set under the crags of a low forehead and knitted eyebrows. His head's shaven, too. Standard hired muscle. Generic bouncer type. I'd never spot him in an ID parade of meatheads who stand outside pubs and clubs in black coats on a Friday or Saturday night.

'I'm not telling you shit,' he pants as he wriggles and struggles to loosen my grip.

'Tell me!' I demand.

'No!'

'Tell me!' I repeat, louder this time.

'No!'

'Tell me!'

'No!'

'Tell me!' I'm practically screaming in his face now. I'm foaming at the mouth and set my eyes in a manic stare, adopting the methods of the Anglo-Saxon berserkers.

'Speak or you'll regret it,' I snarl.

'Fuck you,' he growls in response.

I land a heavy punch right in his mouth, neatly removing his lower right bicuspid which tumbles onto the floor and skitters across the tiles, resting in a small tarn of plasma and platelets. In striking this blow I sustain a nick to my second knuckle. It's deep and saliva-filled and stings like hell. What's more, the force of the strike throws me off balance and he manages to land a hook to my larynx. I'm winded and struggling for air and he slips out from beneath me.

My hypothalamic-pituitary-adrenal axis suddenly goes into overdrive, powering waves of adrenaline through my system. Supercharged, I renew my attack on my assailant with new-found vigour, a boot connecting with his testes, evincing a howl of pain.

Before I know it, he's on his feet and brandishing a knife while I'm incapacitated, on my hands and knees. He's coming for me, and draws his foot back to land a boot in my ribs, but I manage to roll myself out of the way and he connects with nothing but air. I take advantage of his being off balance and swing my leg round, skittling his weight-bearing and weaker left leg from under him. He lands on the floor flat on his back. It's a heavy sound and the knife rattles across the ground.

He makes a strange elongated enunciation of pain on impact and I'm able to raise myself to my feet and jab him hard in the kidney. I'm about to pin him to the ground with his face to the tiles, make him taste the floor, when he jabs an elbow back and catches me square in the jaw with it.

With remarkable deftness for such an unwieldy hulk, the thug springs up and is out of the door before I can regain my feet. I can hear the clatter of his footsteps receding as I haul myself up. There's no point trying to give chase. He's gone.

Battered and pissed off, I lug myself to the window and see him racing across the street before disappearing into the early rush-hour crowds.

I flip the bird in his general direction out of the

window.

'Bastard,' I curse, rubbing my sore jaw ruefully.

Fucking pussy couldn't finish what he'd started, and wouldn't stick around to give me the pleasure either. I'd've taken him apart given the opportunity.

It's no good, I have to urinate. I move to the toilet, unzip my fly, unleash my manhood and piss hard for 2 minutes and 49 seconds. I exhale, a long, long sigh of relief. The release of pressure as the hot jet of urine arcs into the bowl is nigh on orgasmic. I finish, shake off, wash my hands and head back into the main office. I need to clean the blood off the walls and floor at some point, but right now there's work to do.

## 17

Having checked the hidden built-in slimline safe under the floorboards where I had stashed Jackson's memory sticks and cards and confirmed, to my immense relief, that the meathead hadn't located its whereabouts, I decided it was time to get digging to see what I could get from this new lead. I have to admit I wasn't all that hopeful. My searches brought up all kinds of useless nonsense, although some it was interesting. I was particularly intrigued by the story some guy had put up online about his ex wife's attempt to kill him.

*I wanted to determine the type of poison a former spouse used in her attempt to murder me since I've gotten nowhere with the medical community or law enforcement. I still wander around today over 4 years later wondering what the long term health effects are from her violently poisoning me with some unknown toxin. It was delivered either in the form of a glass of drinking water that she provided me so I could also ingest the Bayer 1 A Day Men's Health Vitamin With Minerals and Lycopene, or the vitamin itself. She asked me to take a seat so she could get the glass of water, and I was to take one of the vitamins from the already opened container. She indicated that she had opened them for me, how thoughtful. I found it odd that she would come up with this bizarre request now, since she was busy leaving for a 3 week visit to her parents in Germany. The timing is convenient also, isn't it? I did think it strange and asked her if she'd like one also to which she paused as though I had caught on to her, which I had not, and she wryly smiled, "No sweety, they are for men". I popped one in my mouth, they were large grey pills, and washed it down with the water she provided me as I sat next to her at our dining room table. The effect was nearly immediate: I could actually hear the sound of my brain crackling in my ears and I really was not sure if it was my ears that were popping or my brain, the mechanical effects convinced me it was actually my brain crackling since I could also feel the popping sensation. My sinuses dilated as though someone shoved two red hot rebars, one up each nostril. It felt like someone was ripping my lungs out through my back, and I wanted to scream as I now noticed I was going blind, with spots dancing in front of my eyes like angry bees. I could go on but suffice it to say, I ended up pushing myself back from the table as I noticed my wife sitting next to me observing all of this, it met with her approval, and she then put her hands together to pray a little prayer as I sat next to her dying by her own hand. I stumbled around later and had difficulty drinking water, it would irritate my mouth, my sinuses hurt as though the membranes had been stripped out and they were bloody, I would pass out frequently depending what I ate, which was not much. I had excruciating jaw pain and even eating soft foods was not possible. I had no sensation of pain elsewhere and burned a forearm with third degree burns on a string trimmer muffler after hours of use and never felt it.*

*I would really like to know what she used, and what damage has been done.*

There were no replies posted in response to the blog. The post had sat there for almost three years. Poor fucker. But I had work to do. I still had a missing businessman to find, and I still had a hunch that I'd need to delve deeper into his son's sudden death to get anywhere near discovering his whereabouts.

I needed a break. I began by pouring myself three fingers of J.D. from the bottle I kept stashed. Thankfully my intruder hadn't broken that when rifling my drawers and cabinets, although it was starting to get low. I sunk half of it in a single slug, then went to take another leak.

Urination often serves to fee my mind, and this was one of those occasions. As the jet slashes against the porcelain, I spy the plastic bottle of toilet cleaner stowed down by the side of the lavatory. That was when it struck me: the common element that linked all of the chemicals found in Jackson Jr's system: household cleaning fluids.

Sodium hypochlorite, contained in household bleach. Corrosive; irritates or burns skin, eyes, respiratory tract; may cause pulmonary edema or vomiting and coma if ingested; contact with other chemicals may cause chlorine fumes.

Phenols, contained in disinfectant. Flammable; very toxic; respiratory, circulatory or cardiac damage.

Chlorinated phenols, contained in toilet cleaner. Flammable; very toxic; respiratory, circulatory or cardiac damage.

Carbaryl, contained in flea-powder. Very toxic; interferes with human nervous system; may cause skin, respiratory system, cardiovascular system damage.

Dichlorophene, also contained in flea-powder. Skin irritation; may damage liver, kidney, spleen, and central nervous system.

Chlordane and other non-specific chlorinated hydrocarbons, also contained in flea-powder. Very slow biodegradation; accumulates in food chain; may damage eyes, lungs, liver, kidneys, and skin.

Methanol, contained in antifreeze. Very toxic, 3 ounces can be fatal to adult; damage to cardiovascular system, blood, skin, and kidneys.

Ethylene glycol, also contained in antifreeze. Moderately toxic; ingestion may cause coma, respiratory damage.

Small wonder Jackson had looked like he was burning inside. So, there we have it. Readily available household detergents. As I said, this isn't *CSI*. No special ingredients or rare compounds here. Nothing that hands us the suspect on a plate. Call me a sexist bastard if you like, but I had a suspicion it was a woman who was behind this slaying. Put it this way, I've been around long enough to justify this opinion. It was more common than you'd probably expect. Cut my suspects down to approximately 50% of the population, too. I'd call that headway.

I lit a cigarette as I glanced at the knife on the desk before me. I could've been killed with that thing. But what could I do? No point calling the cops, that's for sure. And as I say, this isn't *CSI*. I can't hand it over and have them dust it for a perfect print or epithelials. Any money he'd not be on the DNA database anyway. People like that have a knack of disappearing from the radar despite a rap sheet as long as my arm, while innocent people – wrong place, wrong timers – invariably get stuck in the system and persecuted for years to come. The system's fucked. There's not a lot I can do to change it. But I've every reason to be cynical and to do my utmost to steer clear. It's a habit I'm not about to change now. No damage done, so no need to call the insurance company or the heat. Really, it's better this way. leaves me in peace to get on with things. I've got work to do.

The phone rings. I let it run for four before picking up.

'W. T. P. D. A.'

'Chunder. It's Gash.' The twat often mocked my name.

'Now then, you cunt, what've you got for me?' I banter.

'The good shit, you prick,' he counters.

'Hit me,' I cajoled.

'Right, listen up. I'm staying under a bit longer, but I've got a contact who's also under and less known than I am, which is how he's managing to pull it off. He's infiltrated Front Ltd., and...'

'Reynolds' cover company?' I interject.

'Precisely. They're having a major launch for some new contract signing tonight at the Ibis.'

'Ooh, sophisticated,' I roll with a hefty dollop of sarcasm.

'Yeah, precisely,' Roger chuckles briefly. 'But of course it's all horseshit,' he continues.

'I'm shocked,' I deadpan.

'Yeah, 'cause you are. Obviously, the client's real enough, as far as we know, but they've been sucked in and as far as we can tell it's all part of some money-laundering racket.'

'No shit,' I sneer.

'No shit,' Gash asserts.

'So how's this help me?' I ask.

'You're going to tonight's event,' he trumpets.

'Sounds like a barrel of laughs,' I grimace.

'You'll do fine,' he retorts.

'Ok. So, look,' I begin.

'No, listen, I have to be quick,' Gash cuts in. 'You meet up with John in the Horse and Jockey at 6:30. That's John Halstead. You'll recognise him by his...' he pauses. 'Actually, you've met him before. Remember him?'

'Sure,' I affirm.

'Good. Then he'll fill you in on the rest. Oh yeah, and it's a black tie do. No, none of that tux shit, but formal, ok? I gotta go.' The line cuts dead. It's the way it is with going to ground.

It occurs to me that there's no way in the world I can go dressed as I am. I look like a fucking tramp. I've got lipstick and blood on my shirt, which reeks after three day's continuous wear. I check the clock on the PC. 16:35. I wind my watch and adjust the time to match it.

I've not got time to go home and change: there's nothing clean to put on anyway. Most of the stores round here close at 5:30, which gives me just short of an hour to grab something that fits that's passable for tonight. I'll probably tack it onto the expenses. Jacinta won't mind – assuming she ever notices. My entire bill will probably be less than she spends on a weekend spa treatment, or a handbag.

I lock up and make my way to Blarney

Street. It has three or four gentleman's outfitters so I should be able to find one that's open, has something in my size and in my price range. I'm not about to take the piss, and besides, I'm not going to be wearing whatever I come out with very often. I'm not really a formal kind of guy. The first I come to is just closing – early, the bastards. The sign on the door says 9:30 – 5:00, and it's only 4:47pm by my watch. Fine, their loss. Hey, it's Bill Thunder here, last of the big spenders! He's armed with a credit card and a license to spend!

The second place I see I walk on by. The shop assistant looks like he's got a broom handle up his arse and a bad smell under his nose and it's abundantly clear that it's the type of emporium where if you need to ask the price, you can't afford it.

The third place is a regular-looking independent store that sells bog-standard off-the-peg suits. Perfect. It doesn't close for another half an hour and my requirements are pretty straightforward.

'Good evening, sir,' says the assistant. He's polite without being ingratiating and isn't overtly homosexual. It all bodes well.

'Hi,' I nod.

'And how can I help you today? Anything you're looking for in particular?'

'As a matter of fact, yes,' I reply. I'm going to make this easy. I tell him I want a suit, single-breasted, in black, plus a shirt and a tie. I could probably use a new pair of shoes, too.

He leads me to a rail on which some suits

like what I have in mind hang. I try on a couple of jackets. The regular length sits best. His assistant's a bit of a smarm but refrains from any of that 'suits you' shit when I'm wearing the duds.

'Would sir consider charcoal?'

'Nope,' I stonewall.

'Very well.' He pulls a couple of shirts. He's astute enough not to try to foist anything with stripes or in salmon pink and I go for the classic crisp white. I'm easily pleased, as long as I get what I want.

I leave happy, having picked up all the kit I need for £197.47. I even add a pair of cufflinks to my bill, partly because I need to look the part if I'm to pull this one off and not stand out like a sore thumb and partly because I'm relieved not to have had to fend off a whole barrage of sales schpiel and inane small-talk from some jumped-up snotbag who thinks he's superior despite the fact that he works in a fucking clothes shop. You get so many like that. Small wonder I rarely buy new clothes.

I hot-foot it back to the office, stopping in at Boots on the way for a can of deodorant. I douse myself in the stuff while getting changed. It's rank, but will no doubt help me blend in with all the poseurs that will be at the function tonight, and besides, I reek of stale sweat after last night's events, the interminable interrogation in the cop shop sauna and the run-in a couple of hours ago with that burgling bouncer. It's been a tough couple of days.

The phone rings.

'W. T. P. D. A.' I answer brusquely.

'Hello?' an old woman's voice.

'Hello? Can I help you?'

'Is that the dog's charity?'

'What?' I blast. It's not the first time I've been mistaken for the Watershed Trust Association for the Protection of Dogs. Fucking dyslexics.

'The charity for dogs? You know?' the bid quavers.

'No, it isn't,' I snap. I'm stressed and I'm in a hurry. I haven't got time for this.

'But isn't that..?'

'No!' I bawl and slam the receiver down angrily. I don't care if she thinks I'm a cunt. I'm sick of wrong numbers.

I could really do with a shave and I'm considering this and the fact I've not cleaned my teeth in two days now when the phone rings again.

'What?' I snarl, fully expecting it to be the old crone calling back.

'Simmer down, Bill,' Roger's voice sautés over the line with a slight crackle. Sounds like he's on a train or something.

'Oh, you!' I exclaim. 'Sorry, been inundated with wrong numbers and had a whole heap of other shit going down. Plus I've got a hunch but can't get it to hang. So many pieces of the jigsaw and they're just not fitting together.'

'I can probably help with some of that when I get back,' he tells me, emollient, placatory. 'But there's o time to talk now. Are you presentable?'

'As I'm likely to be,' I grimace. I'm anxious that my very thin cover's going to get blown at this function. Staying cool around bollocks-arching business types isn't one of my strong points.

'Good. Slight change of plan. John needs to brief you and is on his way to the Horse and Jockey now. Get over there straight away.' He hangs up.

I check my watch. It's 5:48. I can get there by six if I move quickly, but I have to take a dump first. My bowel's going to rupture otherwise.

I bowl into the Horse and Jockey at 18:05:03, feeling like a new man: I'm sharply dressed, fragrant, and 2.14lbs lighter after an epic defecation.

John is outside smoking a cigarette. I sidle up beside him nonchalantly. I'm halfway down my tab and need to finish it before entering the non-smoking establishment. Fucking smoking ban. The seedy dive Roger frequents is the only place you can still smoke, and of course, it's only getting away with it as long as they can worm their way through some loophole in the law that the landlady's found.

'Alright,' I nod by way of a greeting.

'Alright,' John nods back.

John's late 30s and I suppose you'd describe him as lean and ruggedly handsome. He's certainly lived, and you can tell. He looked tired. Tiny lines pulling at the corners of his eyes and mouth, his skin approximating Dulux's Mineral Haze grey.

He throws his head in a gesticulation that we should go into the brightly-lit night-spot. At the threshold I can see it's rammed with corporate cunts: it's almost exclusively frequented by bankers, higher-level office workers and managers and

130

obnoxious buttholes employed in finance and insurance who think they're something. I can't remember exactly when it went from being a half-decent regular pub to a wine bar / gastro-pub pandering to suit-wearing scumfucks, but the referb had been drastic. That they'd kept the old name had only added insult to injury.

I let Halstead lead the way to a table in a corner away from the bar. We press our way past a clamour of chubby cunts in pinstripe suits who are talking loudly in order that everyone can hear how much money they've made and what business they've brokered in the last few days. I couldn't care less. I bypass the bar, noting the lack of hand-pumps. This is my idea of hell, and the night hasn't even begun yet.

We sat down and glanced around, struggling to hide my disgust.

'You don't look too comfortable,' John intimated.

'Funny that,' I twitched. I explained how I abhorred these gastro-pub type places, but conceded that they were closer to my scene than upmarket restaurants. 'So why here? And why this early? I didn't think the function was till eight or something?'

'It isn't,' Halstead admitted. 'But it's only canapés and finger foods, so I figured we'd need to eat first.'

'Uh-huh. Doesn't explain...'

'Most of the guests are dining properly beforehand too,' he explained. 'I have a lead and I've managed to wangle a meet before the event.'

'Right. Who's the lead?' I press.

'A guy called Smith. Stephen Smith.'

'Do names come much blander, more generic?' I ask, raising an eyebrow and wishing I had a beer in my hand.

John chuckled. 'Yeah, he's pretty generic all round,' he agreed. 'Anyway, he works at Front Ltd. and works relatively closely with Reynolds, and I'm due to meet him here at 6:30 and I needed to see you to tell you this before he turned up.'

I nod. 'Makes sense. Cheers. So what else do we know?'

'Well, Front Ltd. is a Reynolds company, although it's set up in such a way that it's difficult to make a direct link between Al and Front Ltd. – nothing financial, he's not on the board or any of that. Our man Smith, however – who I've convinced I'm at the company as a consultant who's been brought in to deal with some of the peripheral elements of the company and to audit their expenditure, because a number of the top-flight managers have observed that it's haemorrhaging cash, which is of course exactly Reynolds' strategy, and the gaping hole in the pensions fund is no accident, I can tell you – confirms that Reynolds is more than just involved in the company. And that means that he's hiding his association with Front Ltd. for a reason. Well, several, actually.'

'Those reasons being the aforementioned, namely that the company's exactly what it says it is – a front – and that the fact it's losing money is simply a diversion, and that the money's not so much being lost as diverted, right?' I deduce.

'Correct,' John confirms.

'And hence... an establishment like this.' The kind Smith likes.

'Evening gents,' said a besuited buttfucker who appeared at the table. I checked him, then my watch. It was 6:32. So this is Stephen Smith.

'Steve,' Halstead gushes, rising to shake his hand.

'Steve, Will,' John said motioning in my direction. Will was my hip corporate undercover name. I'd forgotten to mention this, but Roger had obviously briefed Halstead well.

'Pleased to meet you,' Smith boomed as he pumped my hand and I almost suffocated on his overpowering cologne. It was as if he'd embalmed himself in Joop Homme. It was as rank as it was gay smelling.

He checked his Rolex as he took a seat opposite me. He really thought he was something, being in the money. But these neuveaux-riches are all the same, all about exteriors. All supposed style and no substance. I also hated eating one to one with other guys. Guys drink beer together, maybe coffee. A club sandwich in a pub, perhaps. But none of this doing lunch shit. And none of this wine-bar shit. But Smith may possess information I want so it was only right I meet him in the kind of surroundings that were likely to encourage him to surrender it. Gastro-pub it was. Good thinking, John.

A waiter with a dodgy goatee breezed over.

'Will you gentlemen be eating?' he coos.

'Yes, yes,' Smith punts enthusiastically.

'Are you ready to order drinks now, or shall I give you a moment longer?' the waiter croons.

'Oh I think we're ready,' foams Smith.

'I'll have a glass of the 2007 Chilean Merlot,' I say. When in Rome, I always say. Besides, I'm trying not to stand out and they only had continental lagers in 330cl or even 250cl bottles at almost four quid a bottle. Fuck that.

'House red for me,' nodded John.

'I'll have a glass of the 1997 Cabernet Sauvignon,' Smith said with a dry sniff.

The drinks came and we ordered food. I ordered the hunter's chicken, John the medallion of pork and Smith called for the pan-fried veal in wine with a side order of foie-gras before excusing himself and making for the gents.

'I never did get the pan-fried deal,' I asided to John, a little more relaxed without Smith's presence.

'Huh?'

'What the fuck else are they gonna fry in other than a pan? Unless it's a stir-fry, in which case it's a wok, but then it'd be sold as stir-fried, wouldn't it?'

'I guess so,' replied John, before talking a long draught of his wine down and having a real time trying not to visibly curl his lip.

'Not much of a wine drinker are you?' I smirked.

'Er, no.' He looked a little awkward. 'That obvious, huh?'

'Uh-huh,' I affirmed.

134

Smith returned and chatted uninformatively about not very much until the food arrived. He and John put away more drinks than I'd have considered wise, but it gave me the opportunity to press Smith for details regarding Reynolds and his operation, and to ascertain what, if anything, he knew of the Jacksons and Reynolds' connection to them. Yes, he'd seen Jackson – Mike and Joseph – making visits to Front Ltd. and talking with Reynolds, and what's more, Jackson and Reynolds were both supposed to be in the same place at the same time – at a large conference in Manchester – when they had both supposedly gone missing. But according to Smith, Reynolds had simply been incommunicado and was due to make an appearance tonight.

Maybe I'd get to meet him and do a spot of digging. Meals consumed and glasses emptied, we settled the bill and left for the Ibis. It was only a couple of streets away, but Smith insisted on getting a taxi.

'I do have to get some cigarettes first, though,' I say. Ordinarily I'd have bletched, but figured I had to at least try to look like a rich corporate scum, and kept quiet instead.

'What about griddling?' hedged John as we headed out towards the newsagents.

'What about?'

'You can fry in a griddle, can't you? That's not a pan.'

'Fuck off,' I growled. 'Pedant.'

## 18

As far as my investigation is concerned, the function proves largely useless, and only serves to wind me up and to remind me why I drink, why I smoke and why I hate social functions and people in general.

As far as a launch of a new partnership or whatever it is goes, the actual point of the event seems buried under an endless tide of smugness, back-slapping, bravado and schmoozing. It's truly nauseating to witness. Stephen keeps disappearing to chat with various generic corporate nonentities. He has to be seen to be keeping up appearances. It leaves me at rather a loose end and I find myself continually scanning the room, desperate to find a friendly face, or, more usefully, one I can press for a bit of information. Anything to keep myself occupied is good. Skulking in a corner alone at an event like this is a sure-fire way to draw attention to yourself, and it's imperative I'm discreet here.

I meander my way over to the buffet tables. It's where most of the best mingling seems to take place, and where people congregate and collide before splintering off in new groups. I decide to try my luck.

It's quite a spread they've put on. I comment as such to a woman in a tight dress who's picking up some celery sticks.

'Isn't it?' she says as she scoops some caviar onto her plate. She makes to say something further but it's unintelligible on account of her having shoved a whole individual slice of frittata into her cakehole and masticating gluttonously.

I go for the cheeseline. 'So do you come here often?' I ask.

She may eat like a pig but she's got curves in all the right places and is well stacked, probably a D-cup and all natural. I'd have happily motorboated those puppies. Under the artificial 'mood' lighting her dress is slightly sheer. I can just make out the outline of her aureole, 2.64cm diameter.

She laughs. It's not pretty. 'Nah, I'm supposed to be starting at Fringecore next week and managed to get a ticket somehow,' she says, skirting the irony of my feeble chat-up and chomping on a vol au vent.

I scan the tables for something I fancy and that I can eat couthly. I quite like to the look of the Armenian stuffed artichokes. These lovely little 'jewels' of artichokes and spicy/sweet meat make an unusual dish at a cocktail party or for afternoon mezes. There's no acceptable way of eating them in a formal setting though. I give them and the rollmops a miss and skip over the langoustines that one obese man dripping perspiration onto the crisp white linen of the table cloth is delving his fingers into. I settle for a mini spring roll instead.

I turn to discover that D-cup's taken the opportunity to move away and is pouring herself another glass of champagne.

'So what can I get you?' a middle-aged man is asking a girl in her mid twenties. 'Paté?' he volunteers, picking up a salted clam canapé and popping it into his gob.

He's beginning to thicken around the middle and is balding at the crown. She's a lithe size 8 and dressed to kill in a little black cocktail dress that has a slash collar and has its hem halfway down her shapely thigh.

'No, thanks, Pete. I'm vegetarian,' she beefs, curling her lip with a contraction of a complex combination of the Quadratus labii superioris, Orbicularis oris, Caninusm Zygomaticus and Triangularis. Her lips are No. 7 Red Desert and her mouth presents a small opening to her alimentary canal. It might be the champagne, but I'd happily stick my tongue in there right now. Instead, the space is occupied by a wild mushroom and tarragon Barquette.

'Ok,' Pete quailed with an exaggerated shrug.

I try to join in a conversation with a cluster of pseudo-sophisticates quaffing champagne who are babbling on about the new relationship between Fringecore and Front Ltd., and Reynolds' name's getting some circulation. I get nowhere, and when the group dissipates I try making small talk with one of the young executives who'd been hanging back in the conversation. He chats about nothing in particular for a couple of minutes. I try a change of tack and try to steer him onto the subject of Reynolds in the hope he might throw me a bone, however small. He tells me he knows Reynolds and even mentions Jackson in passing. I prick up my ears and try to press him further, but I get nothing from him other than a lot of hot air about clients and profiles and implementing strategies going forward other corporate shit. I'm growing weary and struggling to fight the temptation to get loaded on the gratis champagne when John appears. The young executive makes his excuses and heads to the buffet tables.

'How's it going?' John asks.

'Shit,' I shoot back.

He looks crestfallen. 'I've not even seen Reynolds yet,' he sighs. 'I'm not entirely sure what's going on.'

'Could be running late,' I suggest, but I know this isn't what he's thinking.

'No,' he frowns, 'something isn't right.'

'Suspected as much. Something's weird about this whole set-up.'

'Yeah,' John concurs, stroking his chin. 'I don't recognise half of the people in here. More than half. They can't all be from Fringecore,' he ruminated.

'What are you saying?' I press.

'I'm not sure.'

'Handy.'

'Sorry, Bill,' he apologises.

'That's Will to you,' I correct.

He smiles fleetingly. 'Oh yeah. Sorry Will.'

'That's better.'

'Don't worry, I'm thinking,' he assures me.

'Well that's ok then.'

It's gone 10 – 10:18 in fact – when Reynolds makes his entrance. The throng's got pretty loud by this point, with many of the guests nicely lubricated. He's heavily escorted, and meets and greets a few bigwigs as he makes his way almost directly to the podium. I sidle toward the man and his entourage, but can't get more than three or four metres away. Even at this distance, something strikes me as being not quite right, although I can't put my finger on it.

The crowd begin to hush when Reynolds steps onto the platform, accompanied by an anonymous looking guy in a black suit and a burly stooge who looks vaguely familiar and I'm wondering if it's because I've seen him before or if it's just because he's a stereotypical bodyguard type. Suit man has silver hair and sparkly teeth. They gleam in the light as he steps up to the mic and the chatter abates.

'Ladies and gentlemen,' he announces, his voice reverberating off the walls of the cavernous high-ceilinged ballroom. 'First of all, I'd like to thank you for being here. It really is a truly momentous occasion. To be able to welcome Fringecore Financial into the fold means a great deal to us here at Front Ltd.'

I'd done a spot of digging into Fringecore's activities and drawn a virtual blank. All I could find was that they were some kind of private equity company who were relatively new on the scene and looking to make speculative acquisitions. High risk investments with the potential for ultra-high yields, and fast returns. Of course, high risk also equates to exposure to heavy losses if the shit goes down. I'd not been able to ascertain who was behind the company, who was on the board, what else they'd invested in, or, most significantly, where their cash was coming from. I know that people – especially

140

the super-rich – like to preserve their privacy, and I'm all for privacy in an age where it's becoming increasingly difficult, but the Fringecore set-up – specifically the lack of available details about it – set alarm bells ringing.

The sycophant at the mic's really pumping it up, gushing like a bust tap about how wonderful Reynolds is and how he's driven Front Ltd. from success to even greater success.

'Who is this guy?' I whisper to John.

He shrugs.

'And the minder?'

He shrugs again. 'How should I know? They all look the same to me.'

The suit with the silver hair's still speaking. 'Without further ado, I shall hand you over to the man himself, Al Reynolds, for a few words.'

There's a generous ripple of applause as Reynolds steps forward and nods around the room, a self-satisfied look on his face. There's a blue spotlight on him that makes his face look ghostly white, shining like the moon into the darkness of the room. He looks a little different from how I remember him. Chubbier, perhaps. But then it's been a while, and I've only seen him a couple of times, other than in photographs.

'Back in a tick,' Halstead says in a coarse whisper.

I turn to ask him where he's going, but he's already disappeared into the crowd. I assume he's gone for a piss.

There's a cliché whistle of feedback through the PA as Reynolds steps up to the mic and silence descends almost immediately. What it must be to have such power, and to command so much respect. He clears his throat. You could hear a pin drop. It's like he's the head of some fucking cult. What the hell's going on?

'Good evening,' he says, quietly, evenly. 'Ladies and gentlemen, it's a pleasure to be here, before you this evening.' He speaks from the diaphragm. His baritone voice resonates in his chest cavity, but has a shrill, metallic edge as a result of the PA being poorly equalised with too much treble. Clearly they'd blown the budget on the canapés and sea of champagne, because the sound engineer was evidently clueless. PA frequency response should be limited from between 30-50Hz 24dB/oct at the low end, and 15kHz @ 24dB/oct at the top. The bottom end limit can often be set at 60hz or even higher without being noticeable, especially if response is given a slight boost in response before roll off. As Reynolds spoke, he was all top and bottom with the mid-range almost completely absent.

Reynolds' speech is rambling and lacking in any kind of depth or substance. He reaches the four minutes and forty seconds mark when he says 'And before I finish, I'd just like to say one more thing...'

I can't wait for him to finish. It's been a wasted night as far as I'm concerned, although something about Reynolds is still niggling me. I'm growing weary and struggling to fight the temptation to get loaded on the gratis champagne when John appears at my side and gives me a subtle nudge. I turn my head discreetly and catch a glimpse of a familiar-looking brunette with some spectacular-looking curves. Fuck me! It's Jacinta Jackson.

'What's she doing here?' I ask John quietly out of the corner of my mouth.

He shrugs and exhales loudly to indicate his lack of knowledge. 'Perhaps she knows someone?' he volunteers.

I steer him to a recess by a window, away from the main hubbub of the posturing pricks. 'I mean, *what's she doing here?*'

'I don't follow.'

'She told me she was out of town for the next few days,' I tell him.

'Ah.' The penny's dropped.

'Thank you, and goodnight.' Reynolds' speech has ended and there's rapturous applause. I can't figure it. For a man supposedly brimming with charisma, it was the most vacuous, vapidly lacklustre and uninspiring five minutes of talking I've heard in a long time.

'Look, do me a favour,' I tell John. Keep an eye on Mrs Jackson for me. I mean don't let her out of your sight. I want to know who she talks to, and where she goes. Try to find out who she's with and what her connection is, why she's here.'

'Why can't you? I thought...' begins Halstead, but I cut him off.

'I'm not being paid to trail my own client,' I explain.

'I'm not being paid at all,' John counters.

'Fair point,' I concede. 'Life's tough. Anyway,' I continue, 'the point is, I'm not entirely sure I trust her, and I don't think she's nearly as removed from all of this as she'd have me believe. But it doesn't make sense

143

that she'd hire me to work for her to investigate something she's directly involved in.'

'Makes sense,' nods Halstead.

'Anyway, I can't keep my eye on her because I've got to keep my eye on someone else and I can't be in two places at once.'

The applause has finally died down and Reynolds is being escorted down from the podium and through the crowd to a side exit. There are people clamouring to speak to him but his bodyguard's doing a sterling job fending them off and keeping his master protected.

I shadow Reynolds, who's accompanied by his minder and the suit who'd introduced him plus another couple of aides who've joined from their places at the side of the podium, at a safe distance. I'm close enough to get a proper look this time though. Then I realise where I recognise the bodyguard from. It was the hired hand who'd broken into my office and managed to escape – albeit empty-handed.

So he's either a general odd-jobbing mercenary meathead or he was sent to turn my place over for Reynolds, I thought. Neither made much sense. I wasn't even after Reynolds, so there was no way he could have got wind that I was on his case. Or was there? Perhaps this was the proof I needed that Reynolds was connected to my case, to Jackson's disappearance.

Reynolds and his entourage made their exit via a door that was hidden from the main room by a short partition wall. I managed to sneak my way through it, unnoticed by them or anyone remaining at the event.

'You did good,' I overheard heard one of the

henchmen say to Reynolds.

'Think I carried it off?' he asked.

'Sure you did. No-one will suspect a thing,' was the henchman's reply.

'I was a bit worried about the voice for a moment there,' Reynolds said. I noticed then that his accent had changed, was gruffer, a hint of Mancinan. Reynolds had delivered his speech with a southern twang, not London, but Home Counties. My research had uncovered that he was born and bred in Rochdale.

'Yeah, Ray did a good job on the sound and lighting,' another of the men said.

'I was struggling at times with the accent,' Reynolds confessed.

'Nah, you were good.'

'With the EQ skewed and that spotlight angled like that, it made it really hard to really tell what they were hearing or seeing. No-one's gonna twig you were doubling.'

Just then, I felt my mobile phone vibrating in the left inside pocket of my suit jacket. I pulled it out and read the text while I continued to listen to the conversation between the conspirators up ahead.

'A resounding success,' the silver-haired suit who'd introduced Reynolds was preening.

'So all we have to do now is hold tight and build up to the grand finale next Friday,' the first henchman concluded.

The text was from Roger, instructing me to be at 911 Lynch Road at 01:00 hours. There was no explanation, but I figured it was important because Roger never texted me unless it was a real life or death scenario. I checked my watch. 22:21:13. Plenty of time yet.

'Yes, I can't wait for Friday,' Silver-hair cackled, and they all joined in, an evil ripple of dark laughter. Such a cliché.

I was following them along a corridor as this exchange took place, my cerebral cortex pulsating as it processed this influx of information. It was a good job they were too wrapped up in their self-congratulatory backslapping to notice me as I dove between doorways and recesses, even taking cover behind a large potted plant as they rounded one corner. Where the hell were they going?

The next corridor ended in a fire escape. I'd have expected it to have been alarmed, but the thug who'd been in my office and left me with the brides jaw – that was beginning to throb again despite the alcohol circulating in my bloodstream – pushed down on the security bar and swung it open.

I dashed down the corridor to the door just before it swung shut, jamming the tip of my shoe in the way to prevent it fully closing and latching again. We were on the second floor and I inched the door open gingerly and peeked round to see the five of them making their way down the metal fire escape that was situated to the rear of the hotel. I slowly, silently pushed the heavy door open and began to stealthily tread my way in their wake, doing my best to maintain a safe distance. The sound of my footsteps were masked by the sound of their feet as they clanged on the iron stairs, then crunched across gravel toward where a number of vehicles including a black Subaru Forester were parked.

The guy with the silver hair paused to light a cigarette, and put his lighter to 'Reynolds'' cigar. If I'd lacked proof before, then this sealed the fact that this wasn't Reynolds, as he'd quite smoking after a throat cancer scare three years ago. 'Reynolds' turned slightly and caught a glimpse of me as I stood, frozen, halfway down the fire escape. I realised in an instant how exposed I was. There was no-one else around, and there was no way I could pretend I was there by accident.

'Hey!' 'Reynolds' shouted, pointing a finger in my direction.

I had no time to think and made the snap decision to head back up the escape. There was no way I could outpace them across the car-park, and besides, I had nowhere to go, and no idea where the exit was. What's more, they had a vehicle with an engine rated 315 hp and 300lb-ft. torque. By retracing my steps, I could take refuge amongst the crowd. There was only so much trouble they could cause me in there.

'Shit!' I cursed arriving at the top of the fire escape.

The door had swung shut and latched from the inside. I was stuck out there on the fire escape. I could hear the sound of heavy footsteps closing in behind me. I turned round to see the burly bastard I'd tussled with earlier looming closer, a retarded evil leer on his ugly mug.

My biological circuitry flashed into overdrive as the pain of the powerful blow registered. Everything went black.

## 19

I came to in unfamiliar surroundings. I felt groggy and disorientated. My face ached and my lip stung. I raised a hand to my mouth and felt fresh wet blood on my fingertips. I couldn't focus my eyes, but I could sense that I was being transported. A face loomed over me and I blinked a few times. Eventually it swam into view. It was the guy with the silver hair from the function.

'Mr Thunder,' he said conspiratorially.

'Huh?' I groaned as pain circulated through my nervous system.

'We picked you up outside tonight's launch event. I don't recall you having been invited.'

'Oh I was invited,' I croaked, my strength beginning to return as my adrenal gland began firing out its juice, 'but I'm not so sure you were.'

'I don't know what you're talking about,' one of the henchmen says from the front.

I can now see that the bouncer is driving, his ham-sized fists clutching the steering wheel and almost covering the rim they're so big. No wonder he's got the better of me twice now. He really is a big fucker. At least he's occupied with driving. To my left is one of the henchmen, and to my left is Silver-hair. My mind's running in overdrive here.

'Sure you do. Where's Reynolds?'

'We dropped him off while you were out,' the man to my right informs me. He's wearing a black woollen knee-length overcoat, unfastened, and beneath it a shiny grey suit with broad white pinstripe. He looks a tit, and must be fucking roasting. It's a hot, clammy

August night, and even with the air-con cranked up really high it must me at least 26°C in the cabin with the five of us hemmed in together.

'No, I mean where's Reynolds?' I repeat in a calm measured tone.

'You'd better watch yourself, fella,' growls the bouncer at the wheel.

'He's right you know,' replies Silver-hair.

'Fine,' I snap. 'So where are you taking me?'

'So many questions,' the henchman in the front pampers condescendingly.

'That's for us to know and you to find out,' the henchman in the back with me pats.

'Don't give me that shit,' I spit.

'We'll give you nothing,' Silver-hair intimates smugly.

Time for a change of tack. Goading your abductors is always an amusing strategy, even if rarely successful. I turn my attention to the beef at the wheel.

'Find anything good when you stopped by my office earlier?' I quiz.

The knucklehead doesn't reply.

'I could have had you, you pussy.'

'Yeah right.' The driver breaks his silence.

'You're a slippery customer,' I persist, 'but you're not nearly as tough as you look. Or as you think you are. I mean, you didn't hang around, did you? You didn't finish the job, did you? And you didn't actually accomplish your mission, did you?'

'You're talkin' out yer fuckin' arse,' he bellows, eyeing me in the rear-view mirror.

I can see his eyes are beginning to widen with anger. I'm not entirely sure where I'm going with this, but I elect to keep on the same track and find out where it leads.

'At least my arse didn't peg it like greased lightning out of my office and over the street leaving a job half done,' I harangue.

The bastard's really getting riled up now. 'You don't know what yer fuckin' talkin' about.'

'Oh I think I fuckin' do.'

'We'd really appreciate it if you kept quiet, Mr Thunder,' Silver-hair patronises.

'I'm sure you would,' I retort. 'You gonna make me?'

'If I have to,' he replies, pulling a pistol from a shoulder-holster concealed beneath his tasteless suit. So, this schmuck was packing. My pulse rockets to 152bpm and perspiration breaks from every pore. Still, what he didn't know is that I had my own protection, and a pound of protection beats an ounce of lead.

'You wouldn't,' I caution, as incredulous as I am nervous. I try not to let on quite how much I believe he probably would as I feel my sphincter tense. The gun's muzzle is still pointing at the roof of the vehicle, but he slowly brings it down and forward until it's levelled at my face. It's a Smith & Wesson 9mm semi-automatic standard, with a 4.25" barrel length. I can't tell if it's equipped for 10 or 17 rounds, but it doesn't matter. A single slug would be all it would take for me to be a goner.

'I would.' His expression is stony, his tone as level as a bowling green.

I swallow hard. 'You'd not want a dead guy on your hands,' I caution.

'I couldn't care less,' he says calmly.

I believe him.

By now I've weighed things up. As far as I can tell, we're on the outskirts of the city and haven't gone all that far. Assuming they have dropped off the Reynolds substitute – and what else can they have done? – and based on my calculated assumption that I was only out for about five minutes, if the clock on the dashboard is remotely accurate in its reading of 22:41, then we're probably no further out than the inner ring road. Because I'm in the middle, I can't see out properly to get a glimpse of any buildings or other landmarks we might be passing, but I can tell that we're on clear road and that there aren't any buildings lining the road. Looks like we might be on the ring road already. Looks like the dopey fuckers didn't think to blindfold me. The doors aren't locked either. This was going to be a piece of cake. Provided I didn't get shot, that is.

I bided my time until we began to pass buildings again. The road was lined with streetlights, too. This told me we were likely entering a residential area. I briefly considered attempting to create a diversion, but figured there simply wasn't time.

Instead, I jerked my elbow into Silver-hair's larynx. He gasped as the air rushed from his trachea and gurgled as the saliva pooled in his gullet. A second sharp stab to the same spot and he's breaking into a sweat and his eyes are bugging as he struggles to suck oxygen down through his swelling oesophagus. He drops the gun. I see it tumble into the foot well. Relief pours through my body.

The stooge to my right is slow to react, but now he's on me, his hands around my throat.

I can feel my oxygen intake being diminished

and swing wildly with my left hand, drawn into a fist, and miraculously connect with my assailant's face. There's a resounding crack as the bridge of his nose collapses under the brute force of the blow. Blood spurts onto my knuckles and down the front of his shirt, spraying the vehicle's meticulously valeted cream interior with a gunky thick mix of plasma and platelets.

He howls in pain and sends his hands to his bust proboscis and I land three sharp punches in the mouth of Silver-hair, breaking his nose and several teeth in the process. He buckles and I clamber over him, unlatching the car door with my extended right hand. He makes to grab at my clothing but I succeed in wriggling out of his grip as he focuses his attention on his multiple contusions.

I'm at the edge of the cabin now and know that what I'm doing is seriously fucking dangerous. But so's staying in the vehicle. I throw open the door. We're going 55.2mph. I close my eyes and launch myself blindly into the darkness, onto the moving sidewalk.

I land on a verge and roll three, four, five times. I'm battered and I'm bruised and I'm in shock. I remain still for a moment, seventeen seconds elapse. I manage to drag myself up. I hurt all over, but it's bearable. I take it that nothing's broken. Without hesitating any longer, I lurch into a side-alley, out of sight. Whatever happens next, if they manage a swift U-turn, I don't want to be still where I made my exit.

I lumber on in the darkness, blind and throbbing, but alive. I hear the screech of tyres. I throw myself behind some wheelie bins and look on as the Subaru with the blacked-out windows cruises past.

I've escaped, but I know I'm on their shitlist good and proper now.

## 20

I'm bruised to fuck. I don't need to look under my shirt to know that I'm a nasty mass of contusions. I can feel my damaged capillaries crying in pain and the blood seeping into the surrounding tissue. No question that these ecchymoses are going to take a while to disappear. Right now I can simply feel swelling and throbbing in almost every inch of my flesh. I've sustained some nasty grazes to my knees and elbows. I pick some pieces of gravel and a small splinter of glass from my punctured epidermis. It stings like crazy. My new suit's ruined. Good job I can tack it on my expenses.

I make it to my feet groggily and try to figure out where the hell I am. There's a street sign a few metres away. I shuffle toward it, my limbs creaking, the movement shooting daggers of agony around my nervous system.

So I'm on Butler Way. I may as well be nowhere. This information is no help at all. I feel my mobile phone buzzing in my pocket. The gentle vibration is enough to send ripples of pain radiating through my ribcage. I take the call, not stopping to check the incoming number.

'Thunder,' I croak.

'Woah, Bill, you sound rough.'

'Cheers, ya cunt,' I snipe. It's Roger.

'Thought I should ring to check you got my text, seeing as you didn't reply.'

'Yeah, wasn't a good time,' I tell him.

'No?'

'No,' I confirm, 'shit was going down.'

'Bad shit?'

'Was for me.'

'Where are you now?' Gash asks.

'I haven't a fucking clue.'

'Huh?'

'Ok, that's not entirely true,' I clarify. 'I'm on Butler Way.'

'Where the hell's that?'

'I was hoping you could tell me...' I hedge.

'Huh?' he repeats.

'Long story,' I sigh, wincing with pain as the contraction of my lungs resonates around my battered body.

'I've got the time,' he draughts, 'it's only quarter to eleven which means I've a lot of time to kill before I have to be at Lynch Road.'

'Good, then you can find Butler Way on the map and come and pick me up,' I rant.

'Ok. Don't go anywhere.'

'It hurts to move anyway,' I seethe.

I survey the scene. I'm starting to feel a little more like myself. A fucked, pain-wracked and bleeding version of myself, but it was an improvement on the ball of agony that had substituted my body immediately after I hit the ground. There are a scattering of residential buildings: horrible high-rises, mostly falling into disrepair. There's one across the road that's scaffolded. It's hard to tell if it's for refurbishment or demolition. The latter would be preferable. These monstrosities are interspersed with run-down looking industrial units, vacant office lots with 'To Let' signs. Someone's added an 'I' between the two words on one of the hoardings. There's graffiti everywhere. Weeds tower tall. Behind me, warehouses and a gasworks. Neither commercial nor residential, it was something of a suburban no-man's land. Most of the buildings are barely fit for squats. The whole area should be levelled, I muse.

I'm curious to know where the Subaru was headed when I bailed. A large part of me was wishing that I'd remained in the car. They'd have presumably taken me back to base, and to their leader. I was assuming there was someone bigger behind their operation. I remind myself that there was a very real danger that had I stayed in the car I'd have been leaving it a corpse. I believed that the guy with the gun really had meant business. Self preservation is the name of the game.

My mind's beginning to function normally again and it dawns on me were I am. I'd assembled a list of premises Jackson Sr. is supposed to be operating out of, and I'd intended checking them out, one by one, before I got side-tracked with all the insanity of the past couple of days. Now I can remember. There was one by the gasworks.

'No time like the present,' I mutter to myself.

I'm not in the habit of talking to myself, but sometimes it helps to break the silence and to provide comfort in desperate times. And these were desperate times. I'd just had a double brush with death. Now I was going to rummage about in a rabbit warren of partially ruined commercial premises and lockups somewhere between the gasworks and the wrecker's yard. I was unarmed and in a poor state. What's more, I really had no idea what I was letting myself in for. So much for staying put as Roger had told me.

I let instinct lead me. There's precious little lighting as most of the bulbs are out. However, the sky's clear and the moon is large enough for me to see where I'm going.

I have the address locked in my head and I track it like I've an inbuilt homing device. It's a real maze of alleyways lined with chickenwire fences and garages with dented doors covered in graffiti. Some have been burned out and there are gaping holes in the fences. Some of the concrete fence posts had been snapped and the steel cores were splayed out and rusted.

I took a left down the side of a warehouse that runs parallel to the perimeter of the breaker's yard. The rusted carcasses of disused cars stood piled awaiting their fate at the hands of the crusher. It was a dead end. I turned and retraced my steps. Took a right where I'd gone left before. The sky was beginning to cloud and I felt the first droplets of rain on my face.

This was the place. I pass a few battered industrial bins and arrive at a steel door. Like most of the others, it's padlocked. Unlike most of the others, it's not entirely daubed with slogans and tags and isn't rusted into place. In fact, the hinges look to be reasonably and recently oiled.

So, I'm here. Now what? I realise I've not thought this through at all. No wire cutters, no crowbar, nothing. I'm going to have to improvise. I look around me and check my bearings. I know exactly where I am now, at least. There must besomething lying around. Perhaps I'll find something in the scrap yard. There's a gap in the fence I can  easily squeeze through if I need to.

I check my watch. 23:12:17. I'm standing in the alleyway in NW2, 57° E by 12° NW, 300 yards South of the river, obscured by shadows. The 100w light from the dirt-encrusted lamp on the wall 7.2 metres to my left with a vertical elevation of some 2.4 metres gives sparse illumination to the objects which litter my immediate vicinity. Industrial refuse bins, discarded cardboard boxes, a miscellany of other waste. It also lit the droplets of water as they descended past the impure and wavering sodium glow. Moderate precipitation falling at approximately 80° to the ground. There was little to no wind, the occasional gust blowing at no more than 5mph from an Easterly direction. The tip of my class A filtered cigarette glowed briefly as I sucked and inhaled a dose of the tightly-bound, lightly toasted selected fine tobaccos, which yielded a fair hit of its 13.5mg tar / 1.2mg  nicotine contents.

My attention was caught by a low-level rustling sound at 2 o' clock. It was quiet, and fast. Sounded like a small creature scavenging in the bins, probably a large rat at 10 feet. I spun 26° on my left heel to locate source of the sound.

I was temporarily thrown off guard by the sight of the man I'd supposedly been on the lookout for racing toward me. Ground coverage – a rate of some 10 metres per 1.22 seconds. He was armed with a knife which I observed when the sharpened 8" stainless steel blade glinted as it caught the lamplight. He was 6'4", 260lbs, heavily boned and muscular of build. His attire was completely black,

SAS style. His features were sharp, his expression murderous.

The hit-man took a swing at me with the blade in a slashing movement. His right arm was at full stretch, his reach some three feet. The hand that clutched the handle of the weapon was clad in a black leather glove. The thug was too slow and my reaction time good as I dodged the swing with the blink of an eye to spare. I grabbed my assailant's attacking arm and pivoting my torso through 90° wrenched the outstretched limb through into a lock. Despite his advantage in terms of height and build, I obtained the upper hand by dealing the scum with a high-impact blow to his unsuspecting midriff. My four-knuckle strike was as sweet as a nut as it connected with untensed muscle tissue. The fuck was winded.

Shocked and weakened, the hired hand released his grip on the offensive weapon and doubled over as the air rushed from his body.

There was clearly going to be no negotiation here. I had to act first and forgo the questions.

I raised a knee sharply upward to connect with his descending face. My kneecap met at a perfect 90° angle with the bridge of his pointed nose with an approximate force of 152lbs per square inch. There was a resounding crack which reverberated about the alleyway as my kneecap met with his proboscis, the bone supporting his nasal protrusion collapsing on impact as the blow hit. The result was a triple fracture with considerable splintering. 10ml of plasma and platelets flowed from his nasal cavity in the space of the 0.853 seconds it took for the bastard's head to snap back as he gave an excruciating howl of agony. His knees buckled and he fell to the ground heavily, like a sack of potatoes.

The mist came down and I was in autopilot. I put my full weight behind the kick, my boot connecting with his ear. The shock of this most powerful blow to the cranium caused the weakling to involuntarily evacuate his bowels, depositing some 3oz of semi-liquid faecal matter into his undergarment. I dealt another blow to his already bruised ribcage with the blunt toe of my black leather boot. This yielded a sharp crack as the sternum gave way. That's really fucked it.

## 21

My mobile phone buzzes again. Shaking, I answer.

'Thunder.'

'Where the fuck are you?' Gash.

'Uh, yeah...' I begin with a cough. I tell him where I am.

'Ok, so that's the where. How about the why?' Gash interrogates.

I explain as best I can, briefly. 'So where are you, anyway?'

'On Butler Way, looking for you, you cunt. I'm on my way over now.'

Four minutes 35 seconds later and he's navigated his way off road and down the tracks that run through this desolate industrial landscape that are wide enough to accommodate a car. The rain's coming hard now and the long drops descending at a 45° angle, driven by the chilling northerly wind are illuminated by the dazzling headlamps as they shine though the darkness. He's driving on old BMW 2 series from 2005 in silver with an inline 6-cylinder engine.

He drives right up to me and stops with the bumper a mere 7.25" from my shins. He dives out and slams the door shut, his open coat swinging behind him. It's a heroic entry.

With a steel pole I've taken from the wrecking yard, I've been pounding away at the lock while I've been waiting. I've made pretty good progress considering. Roger retrieves a crowbar from the boot of his car and heads over to assist me. He clocks the pulverised piece of flesh lying prostrate in the ground a few feet away. He jerks his head in the general direction of the broken body with a raised eyebrow.

'He's alive,' I say nonchalantly. 'Just. I decided to show him some mercy.'

'Reckon he should get to a hospital?'

'Might die if he doesn't,' I concede, 'but it was him or me, and if it had been me I very much doubt he'd be calling me a bus.'

'Fair point.'

We focus our efforts on the door instead, and in a moment it springs open with a huge metallic clang. We poke our heads through. It's too dark to really make much out. Roger heads back to the car and exchanges his crowbar for a flashlight.

'Were you a scout?' I ask, half joking.

'Yeah,' he grunts. 'And I was born wearing pants. I'm prepared.'

We enter tentatively. Much of the building is part-derelict, but the room we find ourselves in has been decked out like an office. It's rough and ready, but definitely an office, with a half-decent computer, a steel filing cabinet and a pin-board on the wall beside the desk that look s like it may have been salvaged from a skip. There are a couple of chairs. They're a little worn, but functional. Roger and I look at one another and shrug.

'Shit,' I curse, disappointed.

'All looks pretty regular and above board,' Gash exhales loudly.

I'm finding it difficult to cover my disappointment. 'I risk getting myself done in for this?' I feel cheated.

We head through the door at the back of the room. It leads out into a short corridor, off which stand three doors. The first one's locked, but the frame's flimsy. Roger smashes it open with a couple of full-force rams of his shoulder. I'm glad he's here because there's no way my shoulders are up for breaking through doors. Even ones set in flimsy half-rotten frames.

Roger scans the torch over the scene and lets out a low whistle. The walls to our left and right are both banked floor to ceiling with hard-drives and disc copying and mastering hardware.

'Must be a fair few grand's worth here,' he whispers.

'No shit,' I concur, 'no need to whisper though.'

'Can't be too careful,' the Gashmonger reminds me. He's got a point.

'So the question is, what's this being used for?' I wonder aloud.

The answer is in the next room. Shelves, floor to ceiling on three walls of the room, with a computer and printer positioned at a small workstation setup on the corner just behind the door. Two of the walls are rammed with DVD clam-cases. The third is stuffed with mailers. We examine the stock more closely. It's all porn, and seriously heavy judging by the blurbs on the covers of titles like *Anal Gang Rape*, *Bloodlust and Butchery*, *Bloodfucking*, *Torture Chamber*, *Death Penalty*, *Asking for It*, *Ultrasadism*, *Pissfun / Shitfun* (a double feature), *Rapemaster*, *Ass Destroyer* and *Titpulp*.

'Woah.' It's rare for Roger to be speechless.

'Now it's all coming together,' I say, rather less surprised. The web was definitely pulling tighter now but I still couldn't see the spider.

We bust our way into the third and final room. It's all there: a full dungeon set. There are sprays of what look like dried blood on the walls and on the floor. I bend down and touch a smear on one of the contraptions bolted into walls and floor. I take it to be a rack. It's mostly dry, but there's still a slightly sticky feel to the residue that's not yet dried due to the recent humidity.

Roger confirms my conclusion. 'Blood,' he says sombrely, rubbing the tips of his fingers together.

'Let's get outta here,' I say.

I get no argument from Gash. He's taking me to a bar on the East Side of town. We both know the owner. Not intimately, but well. I'm speaking for myself here, actually, I don't want to know about what Roger gets up to. There are rooms upstairs and he thinks it's a safe place to go for a while, especially after my recent spate of run-ins.

'So are you seriously telling me you knew that Jackson was a purveyor of ultra-hardcore pornography?' asks Roger somewhat incredulously.

'Yep,' I punt with a hint of self-satisfaction. 'Well, I'd managed to track down the IP addresses and registration details for a number of extreme sites, and they all came back to Jackson, but at a number of different addresses.'

'But how did you know he wasn't just the domain owner?' Gash puzzled.

'When I checked out the summerhouse, I found a room that had been used for some of the photo-shoots. That was what put me onto the fact he was involved in production as well,' I explained.

'But none of this tells us where Jackson is now. Or why Jackson Jr. got snuffed. Or by whom,' he pondered.

'True. I'm working on that.'

We pull up on Home Street, 536' up from The Nine Squares Tavern. Running a late license, it was still open. Roger pushed at the heavy wooden front door and we entered the dimly lit watering hole. There were only a handful of punters in. A couple of phlegmatic old cunts propping up the bar, and a mixed-sex cluster of younger, less phlegmatic cunts around a table toward the back of the room.

'Hello boys,' Violet smiled a cherry ice cream smile from behind the bar.

'Evening,' we nod in unison. I don't return the smile. It hurt too much.

Violet's the landlady. She's roughly the same age as me, but she's wearing well. She's still classic bar totty, with smouldering good looks and a figure to die for. She checks me out and gives me the up-and-down. She wrinkles her face in an expression of pain. 'What happened to you?' she asks.

'What didn't?' I wince in reply.

'What'll it be? The usual?'

'I'll skip the beer and go straight for the hard stuff,' I say.

She pours two double J.D., one with ice, one without. We both knock them back and immediately she replenishes the glasses. Yes, we come here often.

As I'm sipping my second drink, a woman appears at the end of the bar and perches on a stool. She must've been in the toilets, as I'd not noticed her when we arrived. And I would have definitely noticed her. She's petite, wearing a tight top and a short skirt, vaguely slutty but still classy looking at the same time. She's dressed to kill and I wonder whose benefit it's for. She has long blonde hair and a figure to die for. She orders herself a G&T.

I nod to her, and she smiles back. Roger vacates his stool and goes for a slash, leaving me alone with her and the phlegmatic old cunts at the far end of the bar.

'Bill, this is Hannah,' Violet interjects, saving me the awkwardness of forcing an introduction.

'Please to meet you,' I say, raising my glass to the palindromic stunna.

'And you,' she says. 'I hope you don't mind me asking, but...' she looks a little embarrassed. 'What happened to you?'

'Um, got in a bit of a fight,' I hedge, not wanting to give too much away.

She pouts. Rimmel 262, Burning Desire. I like it. 'You look like you should be in hospital,' she says, a concerned look on her pretty face.

We chat. Turns out she's recently single. Her ex is a player and a real scumbag to boot. Some of the things she's telling me are setting off alarm bells. I need to know more. I finish my drink and order another, plus a G&T with ice and a slice for her. The lubrication of a drink or two ought, in theory, to loosen off some of the armour, and then it's in for the kill: hack, hack, hack. A neat slice from the midriff to the solar plexus. Part the dermal curtains of social front and then begin the operation, routing to the heart of the matter. Cut the fat, split the ribcage, separate out the component parts. Haul out those entrails, give those vital organs the close inspection they so deserve. Part spleen from sinew, colon from intestine... severance of blood and bone, muscle and matter, see it all stretched out. Watch her spill. That was the intention. It was not borne out of cruelty, merely a thirst for knowledge. Then I would know. Roger's been gone a long time. Eventually he reappears.

'Gotta run,' he says. 'Laters.' With that he is gone.

Hannah tells me she's staying in one of the rooms here at The Nine Squares. She's been there a week or so while she gets her head together, and is keeping the room on indefinitely. She likes being somewhere her ex won't think to look. She offers to look at my wounds and suggests I rest up for a while. I'm tired and sore. I don't argue. It's the best offer I've had in a very long time.

She leads me up the stairs. My eyes follow her ass. She has long, shapely legs leading up to it. She helps me out of my ragged, torn jacket and my shredded shirt, then heads to the bathroom to fetch some water, some cotton wool and TCP. She's well prepared.

'I'm a bit OCD,' she explains somewhat embarrassed.

'Oh I think everyone has an obsessive facet to their psyche,' I reassure her.

Even the water stings on contact with my skin.

I'm covered in scratches, abrasions, contusions and even deeper, seeping wounds. I probably need stitches.

I go to take a pee. The pungent aroma of bleach is strong in here. I know Violet keeps the rooms clean, but it's truly overpowering in here. My eyes and nasal cavities begin to sting. I check the bathroom cabinet. It's nothing if not well stocked.

As I'm washing my cut hands, I'm still looking for the solution. I clock sight of the man in the mirror. I barely recognise myself. I look utterly fucked. I haven't slept in three days. I've bathed in nothing but sweat. I'm not complaining, it's just how it is, when there's a work to do, when there's a job to be done. I do what I do. I pass silently through. I'm the man without a face. But I got a rep. I'm not known as The Bastardizer purely for fun. Men get in my way, I make their offspring bastards. I don't like it, it's just a part of the job. Collateral damage. Avoiding trouble is easy: don't fuck with me. I'm The Bastardizer.

I return to the bedroom and sit on the edge of the bed. It feels good to sit somewhere soft. The lighting is mellow and the bed and Hannah both look warm and inviting. She eases me out of my tattered trousers. My knees are a mess of purple blotches and dried blood punctuated with the punctures of pieces of glass and gravel. As she's cleaning me up, her face comes close to mine. I can smell her scent, her hair as it tumbles over her shoulders. She presses her lips to mine, then slowly pushes me back down onto the bed.

Slowly, gently, she climbs onto me and hitches her skirt. She guides my shaft, the erectile tissue suddenly engorged with blood, between her dripping labia. She lifts her top over her head and unleashes her breasts – 32B and nicely shaped and topped with long, hard nipples – and I cup them with my hands. She holds my hips between her lithe thighs and grips my girth with her lips. I hold out as long as I can. It isn't long before I release my warm injection, 10cc of hot spunk spurting against her cervix. She moans in delight as a wave of orgasms wracks her supple body.

Sex and money, sex and money... yeah, sometimes I get both. I'm asleep in minutes.

## 22

I awake with a start. Sunlight is streaming in through the window. I'm lying naked in a strange bed. It takes me a moment to realise where I am. Then I remember the last night. I've no idea where Hannah is, but she's nowhere to be seen. I ease myself up gingerly and make myself a cup of tea with the room's facilities. I feel like crap, my body feels like it's been run over by a steam-roller. I drink some of the tea but I'm struggling to stay awake. My eyelids are heavy and I can't fight it.

When I next wake darkness is falling outside.

'Shit!' I exclaim, realising I've lost the whole day.

I race out of bed. There's a pair of trousers, a shirt and some socks at the foot of the bed, all my size and all new. I don't stop to wonder where they've come from, I just know I need to get out and get on, so I pull them on and head downstairs to the bar where I can hear a commotion kicking off by the pool table.

Roger's in the centre of it, and he's got Hannah in his face. She's got a murderous expression on her face. It isn't so pretty. She's got a broken bottle in her hand and takes a swing at Roger with it. Because of the height difference she's closer to slicing his chest open than pulping his face.

'Look, just tell me and it needn't come to anything!' Roger is saying. It's supposed to sound calming, but comes across more like a threat and has the opposite of the desired effect of diffusing he situation.

Not that it would make any difference. Hannah's like an animal, a frenzied mass of anger and violence. She's screaming at him unintelligibly. She actually manages to catch Gash with a flying fist and he's plainly surprised by the force of it. She goes for him again with the bottle and no-one's got the balls to break this fracas up. Me, I know better than to impinge on Roger's territory. Says being 'rescued' emasculates him. Macho prick.

Hannah swings again and Roger ducks and rolls, grabbing a pool cue as he does so. In a single deft manoeuvre, he's back on his feet with the cue raised and is inching his combatant backwards. She stops when the edge of the pool table obstructs her retreat. Roger continues to advance. There's nowhere for her to go, so she slowly inches herself up onto the table, her face now a mask of rage mixed with fear.

Roger lofts the cue and angles the handle toward her mons pubis. As she lifts her leg to attain a higher position on the table, her short denim skirt rides up. She's not wearing any panties. Her beaver is on full display. I can barely look as he jams the cue hard into her snatch. The air is rent with a scream of agony. There are groan, gasps and squeals from those present as blood spurts across the room. There's high-velocity spatter on the opposite wall. Plasma and platelets spill over the green baize as he pulverizes her pussy. It's time to go.

Nineteen minutes and forty-three seconds later I'm in my office. I could use a coffee, but not nearly as much as I could use a drink. I pour out three fingers of J.D. and knock it back in two.

The phone rings. I snatch the receiver from its cradle. 'Thunder.' Better not be a wrong number. I'm not in the mood.

'You bastard,' a male voice snarls.

I'm not in the mood for this either. 'Huh?'

'You cunt! You killed my father!' he howls, his voice cracking.

'Probably,' I deadpan, then hang up. I am the Bastardizer, after all.

The phone goes again. I let it ring four times before picking up. I'm not sure if I should. To my relief, it's Jacinta. Perhaps I should stick to Mrs. Jackson. She is a client, after all.

'I'm home now for a few days,' she says. 'Home and gone, home and gone, that's pretty much the routine for the next month or so.' She sounds strange. Not like herself. Not like herself at all. Immediately I'm suspicious.

'Ok...'

'But I need you to keep me up to speed with your investigation. I just want to know, you know?'

'Of course.'

'And I need to see you before I go,' she adds. She sounds slightly breathless. Could be the humidity, I suppose. I suspect it's urgency.

'Nothing you can tell me over the phone?' I ask.

'Not really. Are you trying to give me the brush-off?' she sounds indignant.

'Hell no!' I ejaculate. 'I'm just up to my neck in shit here, which means I have to be careful. The good news is, I think I'm onto something.'

Her tone changes. 'Really?' she squeaks.

'Yeah,' I deadpan. 'Not necessarily about your husband's current whereabouts, as much as where he's been.'

'I'm not sure I follow?' she queries. She sounds perplexed.

'H'mn,' I grunt. 'Yeah, perhaps it's best we do meet,' I agree. 'Can you call me back in an hour or so?'

'Sure.' She's hesitant.

'Mrs. Johnson?' I say.

'Yes?' she doesn't correct me.

'Where was it you said you were the last few days?'

'Um...' silence on the line.

'And when did you get back?'

Again a long pause. 'A few hours ago.'

'Ok. Might sound like an odd question, and don't take it the wrong way but where were you last night?'

'At my hotel. Yes, definitely.'

'Which one? Here?'

Blank. 'No, no...'

'Are you alright?' I ask her straight.

'Uh, yes, fine.' She sounds vague, distant. 'I'm just really tired. I've been so busy recently, I don't know whether I'm coming or going. Don't know where I am half the time. Or who!' she adds with a small laugh, but it's an uneasy one.

'You should rest,' I tell her. 'Call me later.'

'Ok.'

I call John, ask him how it's going.

'I feel like shit,' he moans feebly.

'Whassa matter with you?' I'm not sure I really care, unless it's really serious.

'Flu. Heavy. Cold... snot, sweats, the works. It's been days now.'

He sounds pathetic. I tell him as much. I don't got time for pussies. But he continues his whinging nevertheless, without my encouragement.

'My chest is now so bubbly and liquid-filled that I can't lie flat or I'll die. On the bright side, my cough has become much more productive which I hope means that this shit is finally breaking up.'

'You'll be breaking up if you don't get it together and start acting like a man,' I caution him. 'I gotta go. Get your shit together, you whimp. So what happened with Mrs. Jackson?'

'Not a lot,' he muscused. 'She took off with some guy. They went back to her hotel room, locked the door with the 'Do not disturb' sign out.'

'Hmm. Cheers for that.'

I kill the call. I've work to do.

I fire up the PC and run through all of the live feeds on Jackson's multitudinous websites. DeathPenalty.com appeared to be closed, but there was a clock counting down to the next live show and some stills from previous ones. They were grainy-looking vidcaps of torture scenes. According to a floating JavaScript, the next show would be the last and promised to be the ultimate finale. Squinting to make out any useful details from the pixellated images, I can't be entirely sure, but I think I know who the two male figures with hoods over their heads are. I feel sick to the pit of my stomach as I realise what the finale will be. I hope I'm wrong. But I'm rarely wrong. About anything. I run the domain again on domaincrawler.com and verify the IP and other essential details. I had a hunch. And I hadn't much time.

I need to check out some files and records that I suspect are at Jackson Sr.'s office. I know it's open 24 hours. These PR people never stop. There's no way I'm going to get permission to waltz in there and rifle the belongings of a missing man, so there's only one thing for it. Stealth.

I stroll a few streets to where I'd left the car parked and drive over to the head office of Tabloid Junkies. I park up on the street around the corner, out of sight of the office and make my way to the entrance on foot. I look suitably businesslike in my new clothes, and I've picked up my jacket from my office, where I'd also found a tie lurking in the bottom drawer of my desk.

Out front, two security guards stand, wearing navy coloured uniforms consisting of parallel-legged trousers, black steel-toes Doc Martens and puffa jackets emblazoned with the firm's badges and decals. The one on the left as I faced them was the taller of the two. Very tall, in fact, 6'3", maybe even 6' 4" but gangly and lacking in bulk, probably no more than 196lbs. Even that was probably a generous estimate, given the bulk of the jacket. The shorter one was stockier: probably about the same weight, but a good seven or eight inches shorter. His eyes were deep-set, his forehead low. He had craggy features, thick eyebrows and wore a stern expression with a vaguely manic look in his eye. The kind of guy I might not fancy my chances with in a drunken brawl: he looked like he could be unpredictable. They both looked bored.

'She's pretty hot, don' ya think?'

'Yeah, not bad. Bit of a fat arse though, and not in a good way.'

'What good way is there to 'ave a fat arse? Freak.'

'C'mon, you know.'

'No, I really fuckin' don't. What's wrong with you? Are you fuckin' gay or summat? That's a fine booty. I'd sure as hell hang out the back of 'er.'

'Fuck off am I gay. I'm not saying I'd not breed in her mouth, I'm just saying I don't rate her arse all that much.'

'Don't take 'er up the arse then, gayboy.'

'Fuck's sake, don't be a cunt.'

There was a pause. The shorter one glanced around in some feeble show of being attentive and therefore fulfilling his job description. Some hope. The taller one looked down at his feet, a strange, strained expression on his long, malformed face. The shorter one looked at him quizzically.

''Ere, you keffed?' he asked.

The tall one turned to him slowly, incredulity on his warped visage. 'What the fuck? Are you having a laugh? No I fuckin' haven't! Must be you!'

'Definitely not me. Smells of spunk,' the

shorter one shot back barely skipping a beat.

'Huh?'

'You take it up the arse and shit spunk. Your farts smell of jack,' he explained nonchalantly.

'You're so full of shit,' the tall one replied, rankled.

These retards wouldn't pose too much of an obstacle after all. It wouldn't take much to distract what little attention they had.

Right on cue, a hen party who have managed to stumble off the beaten track totter round the corner. They're dressed in hideous matching short pink dresses that most of them are too fat for. Their outfits are accessorised with fluffy bunny ears. They look fucking ridiculous. They honk loudly and are all clearly pissed as farts.

''Ere,' one bellows across at the security guards. 'Where are we?'

'Yeah, we're lost!' the fattest one – a size 28 behemoth and a myocardial infarction waiting to happen – brays, then falls off her three-inch heel.

'Where it is you're after?' the tall guard asks.

'Cock!' parps a bottle-blonde harridan.

''Ee said where, not what!' guffawed the heifer, still struggling with her shoe.

'Wanna see my tits?' foghorns the forty-something bleached blonde footballer's wife.

The security guards don't get a chance to decide as she pulls down the straps of her dress and exposes a pair of stretch-marked hooters that hang down like socks with tennis balls in, topped with huge 3" puckered, pigmented salami nipples.

I take the opportunity to slip past them and into the building unnoticed. I stride up the stairs to Jackson's office on the fifth floor, two at a time. The door's locked, but I manage to unlatch it in 4.26 seconds with a credit card. Yes, it really does work, at least on certain doors.

Once inside, I'm looking for two things. First, I check the phone. Jackson has one of those clunky networked Cisco office phones that shows the numbers of incoming calls and also stores all calls made, missed and received in the menus accessible from the keypad. As I'd thought, there had been a lot of calls to and from the same number, which also tallied with one of the numbers linked to one of the porn sites Jackson ran.

Next I located his personal diary. Bingo! His last appointment before he disappeared – based on when he stopped answering his mobile – was with Reynolds. And it was set to be at the address the site was registered to. It wasn't a registered office of either of them, and wasn't one of Jackson Jr.'s either. This was bad, real bad.

I heard footsteps approaching in the corridor outside. They approached the door slowly and deliberately. My pulse rose to 130bpm and my adrenal gland began to pump its juices into my system at an increased level. I froze, then, realising I had to act, tucked myself behind the desk. The steps stopped directly outside the door. There was a cough from the other side of the panel. Shuffling of feet.

To my relief, the footsteps resumed, and receded in the direction they had come from. I got to my feet and raced to the door. I opened it slightly, just enough to peer round into the corridor and see the owner of the feet. One of the night security on patrol. Just because the offices were open didn't mean that there were many workers in tonight. The place seemed deserted. Almost. At the other end of the corridor, I heard the whirr of a photocopier. I could just make out a young woman in the room at the end, standing by the copier, side-on to me. On the wall opposite Jackson's office was a sign indicating that the exit was in the direction of the photocopier.

I decide to chance it and head toward this exit, not wanting to have to worry about being hassled for my ID pass by the bozos on the front door. Chances are the woman wouldn't see me anyway, and if she did, well I'd just have to blag it.

I make it to the door unnoticed, race down the back stairs and in 57.2 seconds, I'm in the staff car park at the back of the building. I'm just getting my bearings and deciding which direction my car is parked in when my phone buzzes. It's Roger.

'Where are you?' he asks.

'Tabloid Junkies' HQ,' I tell him.

'Then I'm on my way over,' he says. 'Don't go anywhere.'

'Wait,' I cut in. 'What the fuck was that?' I demand angrily.

'What?'

'In the bar!' I explode.

'You know exactly what it was,' he asserts. He's right.

'But did you have to go for the full cuntal

lobotomy?' I beseech.

'It was the only way. And it worked. I've got a *lot* of news.' He almost sounded remorseful for a second.

'Tell me on the way to the warehouse down Fetter Lane. We have to get there. And fast.'

## 23

'So she came clean in the end,' Gash is telling me as he drives. 'She got pissed off when Reynolds dumped her.' He's talking about Hannah James. 'But the thing is, he dumped her because he rumbled her having an affair with Jackson.'

'Which one?'

'Here's where it gets good,' Gash smirked.

'Hit me,' I say.

'Both.'

'What the hell? What is it with old man Jackson?' I'm incredulous. Perhaps a touch jealous, too, if I'm honest. He's the wrong side of fifty-five and has girls like Jacinta and Hannah queuing up, it doesn't seem fair. Then I remind myself of the run of luck I've had lately, before it dawns on me that I've unwittingly put myself in the line of trouble from him if he ever found out. If he lives.

'Money,' Roger says plainly.

'Of course.' Sex and money. 'Surely you got more than that from her. That's nowhere near enough to make the move you pulled justified.'

'Oh I got more,' Gash preened.

'She'd rumbled the porn operation. She'd befriended one of Reynolds' exes who said that he'd tried to convince her to feature in a photo-shoot. She wasn't up for it so he drugged her up to the eyeballs so she was practically comatose and...'

'Filmed someone having sex with her while she was out cold,' I concluded darkly.

Gash looked surprised. 'How did you guess?'

'No guess. I've done my research.'

'Ah. For a moment I thought you were going to say...'

'Don't. I may not have entirely mainstream tastes but come the fuck on!' He might've been joking but sometimes Gash simply went too far to be funny in any context.

'Sure. This is serious shit.'

'No shit. So what did she do once she knew?'

'She came down to one of the shoots. In secret, of course. Turns out Jackson and Reynolds, who were running the operation jointly, used to do their own private shoots. The one she stumbled upon was one such shoot. Reynolds was the star of this one.'

'Nasty.'

'Yeah. Especially as he was getting down to a bit of S&M with Joseph.'

'Jackson?'

'Yes.

'Fucking hell. But I still don't see...'

'She was being followed by someone Reynolds had shafted over on another business deal,' Gash pontificated. He really was loving his work.

'Lemme guess. This shafted competitor currently drives a Subaru Forester 2.5 XTEn in Obsidian Black Pearl, which comes with 17" alloy wheels?'

'Spot on, sir,' congratulates Gash. 'You're pretty good.'

'These guys started blackmailing Reynolds and James independently of one another over various footage they'd obtained by hacking into Reynolds' hard drive. But they didn't stop there.'

'I didn't think that was likely.'

'They were – and are – big into research into mind-control experiments. Entirely self-funded, completely illegal. And because they're not legit, they have to obtain subjects for trial by other means. Mostly illegal immigrants and tramps and the like. They've been having their trial subjects running their errands and generally doing their dirty work for ages now. It's a whole new direction in organised crime. And of course, anyone who looks like becoming a liability is entirely expendable and won't be missed anyway. And that's when they punt them off to Jackson.'

'And that's where he gets the stars of his websites,' I deduce.

'That's pretty fucked,' he exhales.

'No shit,' I agree. 'Wait...' My mind's running overtime now. 'I think that could explain why Jacinta Jackson was at the Front event last night, but seemingly had no recollection of it when I spoke to her this evening.'

'What are you saying?'

'These mind-controllers have been abducting her, pumping her with drugs and sending her off on missions. They feed her different identities and she doesn't even know who she is when she's doing their bidding. Jacquie Jobson is Jacinta Johnson is Jacinta Jackson, and she was the one who administered Jackson Jr.'s fatal dose of household chemicals. It was the toxic cocktail of choice because it would point us towards Hannah James. The guy behind the operation would've known about her OCD because he did his research. And besides, she was pretty obvious about it.'

'So what exactly are we hoping to find here?'

Gash grills.

'We're hoping to find Jackson so I can take a bow and claim my fee from his missus. I'm not so sure that's what we're expecting to find, though,' I grimace.

'Ok, and what are we expecting to find?' he griddles.

'Carnage,' I sock to him. 'Blood, gore, torture and the centre of a porn ring, the hub of an empire. This meeting was a set-up. Jackson and Reynolds were lured here and whoever it is behind the operation plans to play them at their own game, so to speak.'

'I fucking love my job,' he sizzles with an enthusiasm that isn't entirely feigned or sarcastic.

We pull into Fetter Lane. Roger applies the breaks hard and swerves the car into a space in front of a garage clearly marked 'No Parking. 24 Hour Access Required.' Fuck it, there's no time to find another parking spot. Roger passes me a gun – a .45 – and I tuck it into my waistband in the absence of a holster. Armed, we're ready to roll. Fuck knows what we'll find.

'Time is it?' he asks as we bail out of the vehicle.

'23:51,' I wheeze. My chest still hurts when I exert myself. I suspect I've bruised the vertebro-costal bones in my ribcage, as well as my sternum. It's too dark to be sure, but it looks like a black Subaru Forester parked a little further up the road. 'Let's hope this is still a rescue mission.'

We scurry round the building in search of an entrance. The windows are high and have steels bars over them on all three floors. The ground floor windows are shuttered on the inside, too. It's impossible to see in.

There's a small courtyard to the rear of the building, and off that is a door. It's dark and the shadows of the buildings on accentuate the darkness. As our pupils dilate to allow maximum light to refract onto our retinas, it's possible to make out more detail.

Roger tries the door handle. The door is firmly shut and appears to be bolted from the inside. The windows all have metal grills in front of them, too.

'Shit,' he vents, frustrated.

'Wait,' I caution, pointing to the side of the building. The adjacent building which sits at right angles to the warehouse is only a single storey. Although the roof is pitched, its angle isn't steep.

'What?'

I step back a few paces. Sure enough, there's a side window. I shin up the rusted lead drainpipe and over the flaking guttering and onto the roof of the next building. Steadying myself, I look back down over the courtyard. Glancing to my left to the building we're trying to access, I'm elated to see that the overlooking this roof doesn't have bars or shutters. I signal for Roger to follow me. He's on the roof with me in the blink of an eye.

Mindful of the adverse camber and the broken tiles beneath my feet, I lead the way to the window. I press my face against it. There's precious little to see.

'See anything?' asks Roger in a low tone.

'Nope,' I reply. 'But don't you think that this is a strange choice of location for a business meeting?'

'No shit.'

'Hang on.' There's a faint light just visible that looks to be coming from under a door off the landing I'm looking in into.

'What?'

'Light on.'

'Got the right place then. Now we just need to get in.'

The window frame's as rotten has hell and the pulpy wood comes away in soft moist shards when I test it with my fingers.

'Lock's feeble,' I whisper. 'I'd rather force it and go in quietly than smash the glass.'

'Smart move.'

It doesn't take much force to bust the lock. The window swings free on its rusted hinges and we swing our way into the building.

A strange odour assaults our sense on entry, a combination of stagnant air, damp, musty mildewed wallpaper and the metallic tang of blood. Yes, there's a heavy hint of abattoir about the place. There are smears on the floors, smears on the walls. Everything's grubby, marked indelibly with years of grime. Most of the stains are of indeterminate origin, but I suspect the very fabric of the building is permeated with subcutaneous tissue, epithelials and the blood of virgins.

I lead the way as we creep toward the sliver of light that plays onto the dark bare wood floorboards. There's a heavy silence in the air but I can sense that we're not alone.

I gingerly make my way to the door and ease it open. I find myself in a large room. It's completely bare, but I can hear sounds through the ceiling from the room directly above. There's a narrow staircase leading off and upwards at the opposite end of the room. I steal across and begin to ascend the stairs, Roger only half a pace behind me.

As we near the top of the stairs, the sounds become clearer. Voices. A horrible cacophony of agony. There's shouting, howling, moaning. The sounds of torture. The sounds of sadism. I draw my gun slowly. Gash follows suite. I cock my weapon. Roger does likewise.

'Shoot to stun,' I whisper.

We nod three then burst through the door.

It's a gamble. We've no idea what to expect. We could find ourselves looking like a couple of gung-ho pricks, outnumbered and outgunned. Or the room could be empty with nothing but a television running a horror movie. Ah well, it's the chance you take.

We've judged it right. The room is kitted out as a dungeon and there are half a dozen prisoners in varying states of ruination, manacled to a range of different contraptions. Two of them are pinioned into high metal chairs. They're badly beaten and only just recognisable as Michael Jackson and Al Reynolds. We've arrived just in time for their midnight execution. There are cameras pointed at each of the installed instruments of torture. Three men dressed entirely in black, their faces covered by horrific masks are making busy with some of the devices while a fourth is hunched over a computer. Over his shoulder I can see that the screen shows the live stream that's being beamed out from the room we're now standing in. There's a lot to take in. In a corner, seated beside the computer in a large leather chair with a ringside position is Silver-hair. Beside him, wearing a vacant expression is Jacinta Jackson. She's wearing heavy makeup and a black rubber dress with the nipples cut out.

I step forward slowly, my feet sticking to the floor which is sticky with blood residue.

The occupants of the room – the ones who aren't bound ankles and wrists – turn with a start. Silver-hair jumps to his feet.

'You!' he shouts, manic eyes fixed on me.

'You!' I holler back.

'Move!' the evil scum orders his men. The first leaps at me, black robe flapping, gimp mask snug over his cranium.

With lightning reflexes, I land a punch in the zipper over his mouth and he falls to the floor with a muffled howl of agony. A second dungeonmaster is heading for me, but falls to the floor before he traverses the room, buckling as Roger connects a spiked mace with his skull. My eyes follow him to the ground.

Horror surges in my stomach at the site that greets me. There's another man lying on the floor. His chest has been ripped open and his ribcage removed in some kind of crude autopsy. Only he's still alive. His heart is still pumping, albeit weakly. Mercury has been poured into the organ's auriculo-ventricular groove. Cameras are trained on him from several angles capturing his final moments for the amusement of a small and disparate virtual conclave of murderous perverts.

'Stop right there!' Silver-hair commands as he sees his men being drubbed and picked off on by one. He has a gun trained on the space between my eyes.

I freeze. Roger is engaged in combat with two other gimps and his gun's been skittled along the ground. Suddenly, help comes from an unexpected quarter as Jacinta springs to life. She lunges at Silver-hair and knocks him off balance. His gun fires, the bullet embeds itself in the wall beside one of the women chained to the wall.

I take my chance and fire. The bullet enters just above his knee-cap and burrows into the cartilage. The fucker crumples. I make my way over to him. He comes apart in small splashes of blood and livid bruises he's going to wear for a very, very long time. Jacinta stands, frozen, a look of confusion spreading across her face.

'What..?' she begins to stammer.

'Shshsh,' I say in a low tone. 'It's ok.'

'But...' It's going to take a long time for her to come to terms with all of this.

I slowly turn and survey the carnage.

'Wait here,' I say. I've work to do.

Roger's already released Jackson and Reynolds from their shackles. They're badly shaken.

'They're going to need a bus,' Gash says, his face stony.

'Yeah. Suspect it's too late for him, though,' I grimace, pointing with my foot at the mangled lump of flesh on the ground. It has no tongue and no genitals and the heartbeat is barely a flutter now.

Having freed the prisoners, I venture into the next room, where I'm greeted by a bank of servers. One by one I flip the power switches to off. Time to close this operation down.